One Year to

Four sisters, four seasons, four weddings!

When their father dies unexpectedly,
the Waverly sisters are set to inherit the beloved
outback family estate. The only problem? An arcane
stipulation in the will that requires all four of them to
be married within a year or they'll lose the farm
for good! But with such little time, how on earth
will they each find a husband? Well...

Matilda is secretly already married—to a *prince* no
less! Now she just needs to track him down...
in *Secretly Married to a Prince*
by Ally Blake

Eve spends a night of distraction with a tattooed
stranger, and the consequences are binding!
in *Reluctant Bride's Baby Bombshell*
by Rachael Stewart

Ana turns to her best friend for help.
But their marriage of convenience is quickly
complicated by *in*convenient feelings...
in *Cinderella and the Tycoon Next Door*
by Kandy Shepherd

And Rose makes a deal with the devil:
the strip of land his family—and the Waverlys'
longtime rivals—has been after for years in
exchange for a temporary marriage!
in *Claiming His Billion-Dollar Bride*
by Michelle Douglas

All available now!

Dear Reader,

This book was such fun to write alongside my wonderful fellow authors in the One Year to Wed series. Four linked books, four authors, four sisters and—of course!—four gorgeous heroes.

At an Australian romance writers' conference, Michelle Douglas, Ally Blake and I decided we'd like to write a series. We invited UK author Rachael Stewart to join us. Fortunately, our editors loved our story ideas!

We were in constant touch, brainstorming ideas for our sisters: Matilda, Evelyn, Ana and Rose. We got so deeply into their stories, we sometimes called our fellow author by her heroine's name!

My sister, Ana, is the secret sister. A "love child," she lived behind a wall of secrets and lies. That all changes when her billionaire father dies and includes Ana in his will, alongside the three sisters who never knew she existed.

It's a tumultuous time for Ana as she steps into the shoes of being an heiress—and a sister. But helping her adjust is Connor O'Brien, the boy next door, her best friend since childhood. When Ana needs help to claim her inheritance, Connor steps up. Can they stay "just friends"? I hope you enjoy their story!

Warm regards,

Kandy

CINDERELLA AND THE TYCOON NEXT DOOR

KANDY SHEPHERD

ROMANCE

Harlequin®
ROMANCE

ISBN-13: 978-1-335-59670-3

Recycling programs for this product may not exist in your area.

Cinderella and the Tycoon Next Door

Copyright © 2024 by Kandy Shepherd

For questions and comments about the quality of this book, please contact us at CustomerService@Harlequin.com.

TM and ® are trademarks of Harlequin Enterprises ULC.

Harlequin Enterprises ULC
22 Adelaide St. West, 41st Floor
Toronto, Ontario M5H 4E3, Canada
www.Harlequin.com

Printed in U.S.A.

Kandy Shepherd swapped a career as a magazine editor for a life writing romance. She lives on a small farm in the Blue Mountains near Sydney, Australia, with her husband, daughter and lots of pets. She believes in love at first sight and real-life romance—they worked for her! Kandy loves to hear from her readers. Visit her at kandyshepherd.com.

To my fellow One Year to Wed authors,
Michelle Douglas, Ally Blake and Rachael Stewart,
for helping to make writing this book such fun!
I loved every minute of our collaboration.

Praise for
Kandy Shepherd

"*Falling for the Secret Princess* is a sweet and
swoon-worthy romance. Author Kandy Shepherd
wrote this beautiful romance which would take
you far, far away.... As a romance reader this is the
ultimate escape. The storyline had plenty of twists
and turns and would keep you engrossed till the end.
Highly recommended for all readers of romance."

—*Goodreads*

PROLOGUE

Garrison Downs,
June, first day of winter

ANASTASIA HORVATH HUNCHED her shoulders and pushed herself back as deeply as she could into the padded leather arm chair, trying to make herself invisible. She felt uncomfortably conspicuous in the grand office that had been her late father's centre of operations at his vast family property, Garrison Downs. The intensely masculine room was furnished with fine furniture and antiques as befitted his status. Holt Waverly, billionaire grazier, public figure, custodian of this one-and-a-half million-hectare cattle station—one of the largest in South Australia—and dead aged sixty-four, tragically felled by a falling tree branch.

It was unbearable that she would never again see her vibrant, larger-than-life father. But she wasn't allowed to show her grief. Her black dress was the only indication of her loss. She bit down on her lip to stop it from trembling and gripped her hands tightly together. More than twenty people had congregated in the office. She only knew one, the elderly lawyer set to read her father's will. But she recognised two others from photographs and media reports. Sitting in her line of vision were two of the three older half-sisters Ana had never met—not once in her twenty-five years.

Ana found it difficult not to stare at Matilda and Rose Waverly—the youngest and oldest of Holt's daughters with his late wife Rosamund. The middle sister, Evelyn, was nowhere to be seen. Matilda and Rose looked like the wealthy, socially well-connected people they were—utterly confident of their rightful place here. Just, in fact, like the girls who had bullied her at the private girls' high school her father had insisted she attend. As far as she knew, they had absolutely no idea she, their youngest sister, existed.

Rose, the oldest sister, tall and slender, brown hair in a ponytail, sat upright in her chair. She looked like she'd just slid off the back of a horse. Rose kept glancing out of the big bay window to the classic Outback scene of red dirt and eucalypt trees as if she'd much rather be outside. Matilda, also tall but curvier, with a mane of blonde hair, sat with her socked feet curled under her on a velvet chair, hugging an embroidered cushion to her chest.

The sisters looked nothing like Ana, with her straight dark hair and slight figure.

Except for their eyes.

Even from across the room she could see her half-sisters had the same piercing blue eyes she had. The same eyes as Holt Waverly—the father she'd only ever seen a few times a year, the father who had never publicly acknowledged her and never given her his name. She was his secret love child.

Her mother had always insisted on calling her a 'love child', when there were other less kind words aimed at children who were born out of marriage to a man's mistress. Her father had met her mother Lili when he'd sincerely believed his marriage was over. Her mother had loved him and had believed she and Holt would be married after the planned divorce. But he'd reconciled with his wife. Neither Holt nor Lili had known Lili was pregnant with Ana when he'd left her. He'd taken responsibility for Ana, but he'd had nothing to do with Lili, except on issues concerning his fourth, secret daughter.

Ana had never been able to rid herself of a sense of shame, fed by the secrecy that had defined her life—no one must ever know who her father was. She hadn't been allowed to call him 'Dad' when they were together on his infrequent visits to Melbourne, just in case she was overheard. Instead she'd called him *apa,* the Hungarian term for dad, as suggested by her mother and her Hungarian grandparents.

And she missed him terribly. For all the distance and constraints, she had adored her father, a larger-than-life figure. Yet even after his death a month ago she had not been able to acknowledge her link to him, her shock and pain at his loss. Such was his importance, he'd been given a state funeral. She and her mother had, of course, not been invited. They'd only seen glimpses of the ceremony on the news.

No one knew about their existence, except for this elderly lawyer who now sat behind Holt's outsized desk. It was he, George Harrington, who had organised the purchase of the house where they'd lived in the inner-city Melbourne suburb of St Kilda, paid Ana's school fees and administered the annual allowance paid to her mother for the secret daughter's upkeep. When Ana had turned twenty-one, she'd been surprised to be told her father had organised an allowance to be paid directly to her to replace the allowance to her mother.

Now Ana was on display in this personal study of the father who'd had such a public life but had kept her existence a secret. She cast her eyes downward to the antique Persian rug. She could almost feel the barbed thoughts aimed at her from all corners of the room.

Who are you? What are you doing here? You don't belong.

A wet doggy nose nudged her arm—a beautiful old Border Collie, its muzzle grey with age. Rather than the usual black-and-white, it was the silvery grey-and-white known as lilac. This must be River, her father's beloved dog. Apa had told her about River, a working dog who had retired to become a pet with house privileges. Now he was nuzzling her affectionately. Did River recognise her as family, if only on the outer circle? Did he sense the tight rein she was holding on her emotions and want to comfort her?

She patted him, fondling his soft ears, loving the contact. 'Thank you,' she whispered to the sweet animal. She had always wanted a dog, but her mother had said a firm no. Animals were too much work and cost too much.

Her mother had kept to a strict budget. 'Your father looks after you now, but we can't count on that. If anything happened to him, those funds could be cut right off. His family wouldn't take kindly to you. Who knows what could happen when Holt dies?'

Ana was about to find out.

George Harrington had already told her that her allowance would continue. But she was required to be at the reading of her father's will at Garrison Downs today.

Her mother had refused to accompany her. 'This is something you have to do on your own, my darling,' she had said.

Ana wished she had her best friend Connor O'Neill with her. She wouldn't feel so vulnerable if she had him there. But Connor now lived in a different state. And they'd argued. As kids they'd squabbled, often about something inconsequential, but had always made up. This time was different. He had a new girlfriend, who Ana didn't think was worthy of him, and she'd told him so. Connor hadn't agreed. He'd told her she'd gone too far and to stay out of his love life.

Ana had found that hurtful. She only wanted the best for him—and clearly that girl wasn't it. As a consequence, they hadn't spoken for weeks. He hadn't replied to her texts telling him about her summons to Garrison Downs. She missed him.

Maybe she'd lost him.

That was an unbearable thought.

Suddenly the dog's ears pricked up and he turned his head towards Matilda. Ana looked towards Matilda too and, for a startling moment, their eyes met. Ana couldn't help a shiver of terror. But to her intense relief Matilda smiled, a warm smile edged with uncertainty but no recognition. Ana smiled a tentative smile in return.

Her sister!

River padded over to Matilda and jumped up onto the sofa next to her. Her sister—only a year older than she was—couldn't be too bad if a dog could look at her with such devotion.

In his wavering old man's voice, the lawyer announced that Evelyn Waverly would be joining the meeting via video call. As he spoke, a large painting on the wall slid into the ceiling to reveal a screen. Ana had to twist herself around to see it from where she was sitting. Then her third half-sister was there. Evelyn was so different from her sisters. City-smart in a tailored suit. Blonde hair pulled back in a tight bun. But she had the same blue eyes as the others—as Ana did herself. Evelyn's expression was contained, even a little stern, and didn't give anything away.

The lawyer started to talk about properties, investments and the robust state of the Waverly family's financial standing. Ana didn't have a clue about any of the business matters, but it appeared her father had been even wealthier than she had thought. The family cattle station, Garrison Downs, had generated much of that wealth.

Mr Harrington cleared his throat, then paused for what seemed like an abnormally long time. The room hushed in anticipation of what they were all there for—the contents of the will.

Finally, he read from the document. 'To my daughters, I leave all my worldly possessions, including, but not limited to, Garrison Downs.'

Ana realised she'd been holding her breath and she let it out on sigh of disappointment. Nothing for her, as her mother had anticipated. But Ana had hoped against hope for some recognition in her father's will. She had only ever been given the crumbs of his affection. It wasn't his money she'd wanted, it was his love, and by not leaving her anything in his will he'd let her know even the crumbs had been swept away. She tried not to let the hurt show on her face.

She had to get out of here.

Mr Harrington continued. 'Let it be known that it is my wish that my eldest daughter, Rose Lavigne Waverly, take full control of the management of Garrison Downs, if that is *her* wish. If not, I bow to her choice.'

Ana looked at Rose, saw her flinch. Surely she wasn't surprised? Apa had spoken proudly of how Rose had helped him run the property for the last ten years. Had he been unaware of how every word praising his 'real' daughters had hurt like a stab to her heart? She'd seen so little of him. She doubted his secret, second-best daughter rated as anything much—certainly not worthy of being acknowledged as a Waverly.

Mr Harrington hadn't finished. 'Ah. At this point,' he said, peering over the top of his glasses, 'could we please clear the room of everyone bar family?'

Ana got up to leave the room, relieved. She wasn't sure she could keep it together. Wasn't sure she wouldn't cry out that it wasn't fair, that her life hadn't been fair, that she'd deserved more than a distant, part-time father. But Mr Harrington indicated she should stay. Perhaps there would be some small bequest for her after all. She sank back into the chair.

Along with her half-sisters, she waited in silence while the other people filed out of the room. She ignored the curious glances sent her way by her sisters and those departing. Perhaps they assumed she was the lawyer's assistant.

'Now,' Mr Harrington said. 'There is a condition placed over the bequest. One that has been attached to the property since its transfer to your family years ago.'

Did this have anything to do with her? Ana wondered. Was that why she'd been asked to stay?

Mr Harrington took off his glasses. 'As I'm sure you know, the history of Garrison Downs is complicated, what with your great-great-grandmother having won the land from the Garrison family in a poker game in 1904.'

Really? Ana wondered how such a thing could actually have happened. Garrison Downs was immense—why would someone have risked it in a poker game? How bizarre.

'Any time the land has been passed down, certain conditions had to be met.' He paused before reading directly from the will. 'Any male Waverly heir, currently living, naturally inherits the estate.'

'Naturally,' Rose murmured.

'But,' said Mr Harrington, lifting a finger, 'if the situation arose where there is no direct male heir, any and all female daughters of marrying age must be wed within a year of the reading of the will in order to inherit the property as a whole.'

Ana stifled a gasp. Although it wasn't anything to do with her, she grasped the magnitude of it—and the injustice. It was obviously the first her half-sisters had heard of it.

'What?' said Matilda.

There was an exclamation from on-screen Evelyn too.

'I don't understand,' Rose said, shaking her head.

Neither did Ana. As an accountant, she had

worked with the beneficiaries of some odd wills but nothing as archaic as this.

'The land,' said Matilda slowly, 'is entailed to sons. If there is no son, the Waverly women *can* inherit, but only if all of us are married.'

'That can't possibly be legal,' Rose said, her voice hoarse with disbelief. 'Not in this day and age.'

'Too right, it can't be,' Evelyn said from the screen. Ana hadn't heard as much about Evelyn from her father as she had about Matilda and Rose, but she knew she was a high-powered PR executive.

'It is…arcane,' agreed Mr Harrington. 'But it has been a part of the lore of this land for several generations. So far as I see it, and so far as your father must have wanted, it stands.'

'How has this never come up before?' asked Rose.

'Sons. Waverlys have always been most excellent at having at least one strapping, farm-loving son,' said Matilda dryly. 'Until us.'

'And what happens if we refuse to…marry?' asked Rose.

'If the condition is not met, the land goes back to the current head of the Garrison family, Clay Garrison.'

Ana, keeping apart from all this, couldn't help but feel sorry for her half-sisters. She was puzzled that their father—*her* father—had let this happen. It seemed cruel.

Rose rolled her eyes. 'That old goat Garrison. He can't tell the back end of a bull from the front. And as for his son Lincoln... If our land, our home, the business we've built, fell into their hands... I—I can't even *think* about it.'

'Don't waste your time worrying about it, Rose,' said Evelyn from the screen, assertive and professional. 'Because that's not going to happen. Not now. Not ever.'

Mr Harrison interjected. 'As it stands, unless all four of Holt Waverly's daughters are married within twelve months of the reading of this document—'

Four daughters? Ana wasn't sure she'd heard right. She barely had time to process what might have been a slip of the lawyer's tongue when Matilda confronted Mr Harrington. 'Wait. You said four daughters. There are only three of us.'

Ana's thoughts raced.

Her father hadn't forgotten her after all.

Matilda spun to face Ana.

'Who are you?' Matilda asked, not unkindly.

'Ana Horvath,' Ana said, getting up from her chair, her voice not as steady as she would have liked it to be. She realised she was wringing her hands together, something she did when stressed.

Then Mr Harrington got up from behind the desk. 'Come forward, girl.'

Ana took a small, hesitant step towards him.

'Anastasia, this is Matilda Waverly,' he said. 'That there is Rose. And up on the screen there is Evelyn. Girls, this is Anastasia Horvath.'

'Hi,' Ana said, weakly waving her hand.

'Impossible,' said Matilda, her voice breaking.

Matilda looked at Ana more closely. Ana endured her scrutiny. As an only child, Ana had sometimes fantasised about meeting her sisters, about them all becoming great friends. Could that actually happen? She was reeling from the revelation she—her father's love child—was an equal beneficiary of his will. She could have expected hostility from her half-sisters, yet they seemed shocked and curious rather than hostile. Was there actually a chance they would welcome her?

Be careful what you wish for.

Ana had wanted to be acknowledged by her father and to get to know her sisters. And now they were all dependent on each other to gain their inheritance. An inheritance that could gift her millions. How did she handle this? How would her sisters handle *her*?

Oh, Connor, why aren't you here to advise me?

Had she pushed him away for good? They'd

grown up next door to each other and he'd always been there for her, warning off the bullies at primary school, letting her cry on his shoulder when she'd been hurting. He was the only person aside from her mother and grandparents who knew the truth about her father. Two years older than she, he'd always been wiser than his years, always able to be trusted. Now, when she most needed his advice, she would have to face this on her own.

She'd had no expectations from her wealthy father other than the continuation of her monthly allowance. Yes, she could walk away from this. But, if she did, her sisters would lose their birthright.

But it was her birth right too.

The wealth involved would make an enormous difference to her life. She'd be a fool to turn her back on that.

'Rose?' Matilda said quietly.

'Hang on. Evie, did you *know*? Is this why—?' Rose began.

'I have to go,' said Eve, looking as pale as the white walls surrounding her, before the TV turned to black.

Rose, visibly disconcerted by the shock contents of the will, got up and headed towards the door. 'I can't— I don't have time for this. I have a station to run,' she threw over her shoulder.

At the door she stopped, turned, pointed at Ana and barked, 'Stay!' And then she was gone.

Stay. At Garrison Downs.

Her father's property had attained mythical status in Ana's eyes. She had always wondered about it. Never thought she would see it. And now she was here—welcomed by her half-sisters.

Ana nodded. But Rose had already gone and Ana wasn't sure if she had seen her give her assent. She looked at Matilda, kind-eyed Matilda, with whom she already felt a tenuous connection. Matilda smiled and rolled her eyes a little, as if to say, 'You know what Rose is like'.

But Ana didn't know what Rose was like. Or Matilda. Or Evelyn—Evie, her sister had called her. But she wanted to get to know her sisters.

They were of her blood.

For any of them to claim their inheritance, all four of Holt Waverly's daughters had to be married within the year. They would have to work together. Ana couldn't be the one to ruin it for the others.

She had to find a husband.

CHAPTER ONE

Melbourne,
December, first day of summer

IT HAD BEEN six months since that drama-laden reading of her father's will—six months to go until the deadline for all four sisters to wed, so as to secure their inheritance. And Ana was no closer to finding a man to marry. She had tried, really tried, only to end up with a string of dead-end dates. In six months, she hadn't met one man with whom she could remotely imagine sharing her life.

But both she and her new-found sisters had so much to lose if she didn't find a husband. Matilda had dropped the bombshell that she was already secretly married—to a European prince, no less. In August, Matilda and Henri had had a grand, official royal wedding ceremony in Chaleur. In November, Eve had married George Harrington's son, Nate. Rose was still single. But Rose was so formidably efficient, Ana had no doubt she'd be married by the end of the year—although there didn't appear to be any contenders yet.

Ana, the secret sister her half-sisters had embraced so wholeheartedly, couldn't be the one to let them down by remaining uncoupled. She was losing sleep and losing weight from the pressure of the relentlessly ticking clock—at the same time dealing with her grief at the loss of her father. Sometimes the pain slammed into her, hard and unexpected. He was gone and he would never visit her in Melbourne again.

But there was anger along with the grief. Why hadn't Apa ever given her some clue about what his will held? And, after his wife Rosamund had died, couldn't she have been allowed to meet her sisters then? She felt sad that she'd gone twenty-five years without knowing the wonderful women her sisters had turned out to be.

Not that her link to Holt Waverly was now any less secret than it had been all her life. She and her sisters had agreed that both the condition of the will and her new role in the family should be kept hush-hush until they were all safely married. Otherwise the media would certainly pounce on the story. Then their lives would be hell.

That was one reason she hadn't told any of her dates about the inheritance her marriage would trigger. The other was that she wanted marriage for the right reasons, not because she was suddenly an heiress. But the more she tried to meet the right man, the more stressed she felt. She was beginning to wonder if she was driving away potential partners rather than attracting them.

With six months to go and no husband in sight, her mother, Lili, had called a family meeting. Lili had been as stunned as Ana at the terms of Holt's will that placed her daughter as an equal to his legitimate daughters.

'He loved you, he truly did,' she'd said through her tears. Ana's grandparents had not liked or approved of Holt. However, they felt Ana's inheritance went some way towards mitigating the way Holt had seduced their only daughter, Lili, with false assurances of marriage.

None of them could understand why a twenty-first century bequest would have such an archaic requirement for marriage.

It was two hours before Saturday evening opening time at the Hungarian restaurant run by her grandparents in the beach-side suburb of St Kilda. Four of them sat around a round table—Ana, Lili and her grandparents, Dori and Zoltan. Two chefs were busy at work in the kitchen. In the early days, her grandparents did all the work themselves. Now they were easing down as they got older. If—*when*—she got her inheritance Ana vowed to help them financially. Refugees who'd fled Hungary many years ago, their early lives hadn't been easy.

The restaurant had always been her happy place. Ana loved the eclectic décor comprising wooden floors, bentwood chairs, crystal chande-liers, art prints of old Budapest, the always pres-ent aromas of delicious Hungarian food and the warmth and welcome. As a child she'd often sat at this very table doing her homework in the gap between school ending and her mother finishing work in the city and coming to take her back to their nearby home. When she'd been in primary school, Connor had often sat here with her.

Her grandfather started off the meeting. 'An-astasia, we can't have you risk losing your right-ful share of your father's billions because you are too picky with—'

Her mother glared at Nagypapa and cor-rected him. 'Because she's finding it difficult to connect with suitable men, you mean?' Lili paused. 'I've been thinking. Perhaps we need to widen the husband-hunt net.'

'The *hunt*? The *net*?' Ana pulled a face. 'That sounds so predatory.' She took a breath. 'Do I seem predatory? Maybe I'm scaring guys off— coming across as too keen for commitment. Too needy, perhaps.'

It was bad enough dating a stranger, but knowing she was assessing them as a possible husband made her feel even more awkward. From the number of guys not pressing for a second date, they might also have felt the same.

'Or the ones who are serious about settling down sense that you really don't want to get married,' her mother said. 'To anyone.'

'Perhaps,' Ana said, shifting uncomfortably in her seat.

She'd thought of marriage as something in her future. Now, at age twenty-five, she wanted to be independent, to live her life on her own terms, not someone else's. The wealth that could be unlocked to her by the inheritance would give her every chance to do that. She wanted to quit her boring accountant job at the insurance company and concentrate more on her fledgling online jewellery business.

Why on earth did that caveat in the will have to force her sisters and her to marry? It was ridiculous and unfair. Evelyn had tried to challenge it, but it had seemed the clause was set in stone.

Her grandmother shook her head. 'The problem isn't you, *kicsim*—you're beautiful, smart and kind. You'd make the right man a wonderful wife. It's these dating apps that you young folk rely on, they're the problem. Who knows what could be wrong with men who have to look for women online?'

Ana cleared her throat. 'Actually, Nagy-mama, they're people like me. I'm on those sites too, remember?' She'd tried them all, swiping left most of the time.

'You're too good for them,' her grandmother said with a dismissive sweep of her hand. 'And there is no substitute for an introduction to a suitable man whose family is known to your family.' She looked at Ana with narrowed eyes. 'Your mother is right. I need to widen my net.'

'Oh, no. No, thank you, Nagymama,' Ana said quickly. 'No more introductions, I insist. You can't imagine how embarrassing it was both for me and the "eligible" guy who was forced into meeting me because his grandparents are your friends.'

There had been one such family friend who had sparked her interest. Then he'd told her he had agreed to see her just to put off his parents, as he wasn't ready yet to come out as gay. But she'd made a new friend that day, so it hadn't been a total waste of time, like the others had been.

'What about letting me help?' said her grand-father. 'My friends at the Hungarian Club are always boasting about their grandsons. I could ask—'

Ana flung up both hands in protest. 'No.

Thank you for the kind thoughts, both of you, but no more match-making. Please.'

'Darling, you've only got six months to get married,' said her mother. 'Surely you should be open to all possibilities?'

Ana shrugged. 'I'm not doing well on my own, I admit it. Perhaps I need help with updating my profiles on the dating apps—you know, to better promote myself.'

'I don't know that I could help with that,' said her mother.

'Or me,' said her grandmother with an expressive lift of her brows.

Ana smiled. 'I wasn't actually thinking of asking for your help. I'm going to ask Connor to help me get a more effective message across.'

'Connor? But isn't he living in Sydney?' said her grandfather.

'He's back in Melbourne.' Ana looked at her watch. 'And should be here to meet me very soon.'

Not long after the reading of the will, he'd contacted her to say she'd been right about his girlfriend and he'd ended it.

'We're catching up tonight.'

Her family's faces lit up. They all loved Connor. He'd lived next door to her mother and her in St Kilda, along with his doctor parents and younger brother. She and Connor had constantly been in and out of each other's homes. Everyone thought of him as a big brother to her. It was why she'd never really thought of herself as a lonely only child. For as long as she could remember, there had been Connor.

Her grandmother got up from her chair and prodded Zoltan into vacating his. 'We must get *gulyas* ready for him. It's his favourite.'

Ana laughed. After her grandparents headed to the kitchen, she and her mother reminisced how teenaged Connor had always angled for an invitation to go with them to the restaurant for a meal. He was energetic, sporty and always seemed to be hungry. As he'd grown up, he'd had his own friends, his own ways of spending the evening rather than with his next-door neighbour's family. But there had always been food on the table for Connor, and room for him in the Horvaths' hearts.

And in *her* heart? Connor was a friend. Just a platonic friend. He'd made that very clear to her the one and only time they had shared a kiss at her Year Ten formal. He'd said it was because they were too young to get involved that way and it would be weird. When she'd suggested they lose their virginities together, he had paled.

'You know I think of you as a sister, right?' he'd choked out, backing away.

Of course, she'd hastily backtracked to say

she'd been joking. But she hadn't been. She couldn't remember when her attraction to Connor had started. Probably when they'd both reached puberty and skinny, gangly Connor had filled out and grown into his height. Or maybe she'd become aware of him in that way when girls from school had wanted introductions to her 'hot neighbour'. But he'd made it clear he didn't see her as anything other than a close friend and she'd had to settle for that.

Ultimately, it had been the right decision. Boyfriends came and went; a friend like Connor stayed in her life. She would never want to risk losing him by trying to push him to be something else.

'So your best plan is to improve your profile on the dating apps?' her mother asked.

'And to continue going to the gym, socialising with people from work at any opportunity, borrowing a dog to walk in the park where the cool guys walk their dogs, enrolling in male-orientated hobby courses...'

'Oh, dear, that sounds like hard work,' said her mother. 'The trouble is, you can't go out chasing love. Love comes to you when you don't expect it.'

'Love? Why are we talking about love?' Ana had been thinking of attraction and compatibility as criteria for the husband hunt. Not necessarily love.

'Isn't love the only reason to get married?'

Her mother had a wistful look on her face. Ana knew she had loved Holt and believed he had loved her; had thought they would marry after his divorce. Until he'd gone back to the marriage he'd sworn was over. It had taken her mother a very long time to find love again with Ben, whom Ana liked very much. Ben wasn't at the meeting. He wisely stayed out of any discussions to do with Holt, or the repercussions of Holt's will.

'Well, yes,' she said.

'So aren't you looking for love? Isn't that why it's proving so difficult for you to find someone?'

Her mother knew her so well, Ana thought. She'd had a few nice boyfriends whose company she had really enjoyed. She'd had one not-so-nice boyfriend who'd lasted longer than the others but had proved to be controlling and domineering. She shuddered at the very thought of Rory. But had she ever really been in love? In love enough to get married, that was. Would she recognise love if she tripped over it?

She sighed. 'Okay, so I should be out looking for love.'

'Or being open to love finding you,' her mother said.

Ana was about to ask her mother what exactly she meant by that when the door from the street opened and there was Connor, framed in the doorway.

Her breath caught in her throat. Connor. The same familiar, handsome Connor—tall, long limbed but, in some shockingly subtle way, different. Different enough for her to feel, for the first time in their lifelong friendship, a little awkward. She stayed glued to her chair rather than rushing up to greet him.

In faded blue jeans and a black T-shirt, his dark-blond hair streaked gold from the sun, he seemed broader in the shoulders, more muscular, more *powerful*. Surely he couldn't be taller? Not aged twenty-seven. It must be the way he was holding himself. She hadn't actually seen him for more than six months; video calls weren't quite the same as being together in person.

Then he grinned, the big, friendly, all-encompassing grin he'd had even as a seven-year-old. With that open look on his face that said he expected life would be good to him.

She smiled back, buoyed with sudden joy, and jumped up from her chair to step near and greet him. 'You're back. It's been so long. I've *missed* you.'

He looked deep into her eyes, as he always did. 'I missed you too.'

Then she was swept up into his arms. 'Your biggest, bestest, Connor bear-hug,' she said, her voice muffled against his shoulder. His chest was hard with muscle. He must have been working out while he'd been away. She closed her eyes in the bliss of having him close again.

Her best friend.

Her mother was next in line for a Connor hug. Then her grandparents were there, bearing steaming bowls of *gulyas* and buttered noodles. They placed the dishes on the table. Connor hugged each of them in turn.

'You must be hungry,' said her grandmother, doting on him as she'd done since he'd been a little boy.

'How did you guess?' he said with that heart-warming grin. He sniffed, loud and exaggerated. 'And, if I'm not wrong, you've made me my favourite meal.'

'Always,' said her grandfather, smiling, not hiding his delight.

Ana knew that Connor probably was genuinely hungry. He always seemed to be hungry. But even if he had just eaten a three-course meal he would still have said he was hungry because he knew it would please her grandparents. That was Connor all round. Not a people pleaser, but a person who was kind and truly considerate of others. She couldn't risk losing him again. The weeks they hadn't spoken had been hell.

'How could such a gorgeous-looking guy be so darn nice?' her friend Kartika had said when Ana had first introduced them.

Ana had shrugged. 'Dunno. He's just like that. Always has been.'

He was super-smart too. It was no wonder his family had expected him to become a doctor. His parents were doctors. His grandfather had been a doctor. And his great-grandfather before that. But Connor had studied medicine at university for one year and decided it wasn't for him.

To the consternation of his family, he'd left, with the stated aim of becoming wealthy. Connor being Connor, he'd succeeded at that beyond everyone's expectations. He'd become a multi-millionaire by the time he'd been twenty-one. Without ever being obnoxious about it, not even for a minute.

Then he'd studied what he'd always wanted to study: veterinary science. He was now a qualified vet doing volunteer work for, as he said, 'animals and the people who love them'. Indigenous animals in danger were his main focus.

Ana knew Connor had his demons—his parents' divorce had affected him badly—but he was the kind of person who didn't want his pain to impinge on others. Sometimes over the years she'd wondered if that reticence was actually a good thing.

Her grandparents doted on him. He'd been part of their lives for so long, the grandson they'd never had. As she watched him chat with them, she realised what was different about her friend. He'd always been the boy next door. Now she couldn't call him that. He no longer lived next door, but that wasn't it. At twenty-seven, Connor was definitely a man. And every fibre of her being was aware of it.

'Come. Eat. All of you,' ordered her grand-mother in her soft Hungarian accent.

Ana realised she was hungry too. The relent-less pressure that came with having to find a husband had lifted. Connor was here. Of all people, he knew best her good points and her bad. He would help her present a more wife-friendly image to the online dating arena. She knew she could count on him.

Actually, now she thought of it, why not ask him if knew of any possible prospects among his friends and acquaintances?

CHAPTER TWO

AFTER DINNER, Ana walked beside Connor along the St Kilda foreshore on the palm-tree-lined pathway that ran parallel to the beach with a view over Port Phillip Bay. She was feeling ridiculously happy that he was with her. In recent years they hadn't seen as much of each other as they'd had when he'd lived next door. That was inevitable. Life got in the way. Boyfriends and girlfriends who felt threatened by their friendship got in the way.

But it had been too long a break from seeing him. Her life had been turned upside down during that time. And she had struggled to work things out without his support.

'It's good to be home,' he said.

The sigh that accompanied his words was uncharacteristic. Connor didn't do sighs. What had happened up there in Sydney? She knew he'd broken off with Brandi, the woman Ana hadn't liked. But break-ups didn't usually affect Connor. He'd always shrug and tell her the relationship had run its course. Then he'd bounce back. He might go long stretches between girlfriends—he was fussy about whom he dated—but there would be another one soon enough. Connor didn't need to chase women—they chased him.

'It's good to have you home,' she said. Mundane words, perhaps, but they were heartfelt. Somehow, already her world seemed on a more even keel.

It was a balmy, early summer evening. Melbourne was notorious for having all four seasons in one day because of its volatile weather. Not so today. People were still on the beach—some brave souls swimming, a group of kids chasing a ball around on the sand.

Connor and her didn't hold hands. She didn't slip her hand into the crook of his elbow. He didn't put his arm around her.

They were friends.

A hug, a kiss on the cheek in greeting, was the extent of any physicality between them. It had always been that way. Except for that one, memorable kiss back in high school. That kiss had started as something light, experimental, but had quickly turned into something deep and passionate and utterly heart-stirring. It was the kiss she had never imagined a kiss could be. The first time she had felt the first thrilling stirrings of desire. She had wanted it to last for ever. If the kiss had to end, she wanted another. But to Connor that kiss had not been the right thing to do. Not with the girl next door. Not then, not ever. He'd made it very clear.

They walked towards a group of buskers playing a throbbing, inviting rhythm on African drums. Ana found herself timing her steps to the beat. Connor laughed when he realised what she was doing and joined in. Then, as they reached the drummers, he swung her into a spontaneous dance on the pavement. Laughing, Ana followed his lead as she lost herself in the compelling drum beats, the full skirt of her vintage-inspired dress swirling around her.

Connor danced with a sensuous, rhythmic grace. A lock of his blond hair fell over his forehead, his eyes gleamed green with energy and enthusiasm. He was, undoubtedly, hot. But she couldn't allow herself to want him. She had long ago trained herself not to be aware of her friend as sexually desirable. Or to think even for a moment what an asset a good sense of rhythm could be to a man. This was just Connor.

Other passers-by joined in, until there was a group of strangers dancing with them. They were uninhibited, laughing, enjoying them-

selves. Ana felt warmed by the good will that
surrounded them. This was fun. Connor waved
to the small audience that had congregated to
watch the drummers and the dancers. They
clapped. Entirely unselfconscious, he bowed to
them.

'Why does this kind of thing only happen
when I'm with you?' Ana said, a little breath-
less from the pace of the dance.

'Because of the company I keep?'

He answered her question with a grin and
another question that didn't answer anything.
That was Connor being Connor. Not for the
first time, Ana was glad she was his friend and
not his girlfriend. He had broken more than
a few hearts, while her heart remained intact.
And she still had him in her life. Staying just
friends was worth it.

The drums stopped. The dancers came to a
halt and they started to disperse, the rhythmic
bond that had drawn strangers together broken.
As an older lady walked past, she patted Ana
on the arm. 'You two make such a cute couple.'

'Oh. I… We…we're not—' Ana stuttered,
taken aback.

'Thank you for saying so,' said Connor graciously. He always seemed to have the right
words to hand. In this case, he didn't confirm
or deny their coupledom, but Ana was saved

from an awkward moment. The woman chose to take it as an affirmation and seemed pleased.

Connor pulled his wallet from his pocket and threw a generous number of dollars into the drummer's busking hat. Ana and he resumed their walk.

'Okay, Ms Heiress, bring me up to date with the search for a husband,' he said.

'There's not much to update you with, unfortunately.' She looked up at him. 'But, Connor, before we talk about what my mum calls the "husband hunt", before I update you on how things are going with my sisters, I want to talk to you about—'

'It gives you a thrill to say that, doesn't it? Your sisters.'

'It does. I still can't believe they're in my life. *I have three sisters!* I have to pinch myself to make sure it's all real.'

'They don't resent you?'

'Far from it. They're upset they had a sister all this time and no one told them.'

Connor's eyes narrowed. 'Surely your sudden appearance at age twenty-five must have been hard for your sisters to accept? Especially when you're making a claim on a substantial inheritance that's suddenly split four ways instead of three. I wish I'd been a fly on the wall at the reading of the will.'

'I wished you'd been there too—not as a fly but as you. It was quite scary.' If only she'd been able to have even a phone call with him, she would have felt better about facing the challenges Apa's will presented. 'Rose and Tilly must have been shocked but they graciously welcomed me, they really did. I expected hostility but I got hospitality instead.'

'Tilly?' he said.

'That's what Rose and Eve call Matilda. She asked me to call her Tilly too. And Evelyn is Evie, or Eve.'

'That's very nice, isn't it?' His tone laced his words with something less than positivity.

'Please don't sound so cynical. They truly are wonderful women.'

'Because they need you on side so they can claim their inheritances.'

'There's that, I suppose.' She paused. 'But I believe they're genuine in their welcome to me.'

'What about the sister in London?'

'I met Eve when she came back to Australia to visit in September. She turned out to be just as lovely as the other two. She came and had dinner at the restaurant with me and my family. We had a surprise visit from Nate, too, which was very romantic.'

'That's significant?'

'Absolutely. I was anticipating disaster. After

all, when you come down to the truth of it, my mum had an affair with her dad. He had another child his family knew nothing about. Can you imagine? Eve accidentally found out about the affair when she was a teenager. As a result, she became estranged from the family and very bitter towards her father. But it seems she no longer holds a grudge against my mother, and we all got on really well. Even my grandparents fell for Eve and Nate. They're family now. Mum was nearly in tears by the end of it. Even though she genuinely believed Holt was getting divorced when she got together with him, she always felt she'd wronged the Waverly family.'

'I'm glad Eve doesn't blame you for what happened with your parents,' he said. 'The sins of the fathers and all that.'

Ana rolled her eyes. 'Literally the sins of my father. Who knows why he let my mother believe he would marry her? Tilly was only a tiny baby at the time.'

Connor was the only friend with whom she could talk about her father in any depth. And it still felt weird to think about Holt and Lili as lovers. Who ever wanted to think about their parents in that way?

'Simple. It was a sure-fire way of getting her into bed. I can't imagine gorgeous Lili would have been an easy seduction.'

She gasped. 'Connor! That's going too far.' She shuddered. 'That's my mother you're talking about.'

'It's a guy thing.' He shrugged. 'You know what they say—a horny guy has no conscience. Love. Commitment. Marriage: He'll spin any yarn if he thinks it's what she wants to hear. Anything to get him into a girl's pants.'

'Stop! I don't want to know your seduction techniques.' She paused. 'Have you ever—? No. I really don't want to know.'

He laughed. 'You rise to the bait every time.'

'And you're such a tease,' she said, smiling in spite of herself.

'I try,' he said with that irrepressible grin.

'I prefer to believe that Holt genuinely loved my mother. But circumstances at home changed and he made the right choice for his family. Remember, they didn't know Mum was pregnant with me at the time they ended their relationship.'

'But he took responsibility for you. Tried to maintain a relationship.'

'It was never enough. I was just getting to know him again and I'd be waving him goodbye.'

'I remember how sad you'd be after he left. But he made it up to you at the end with his will.'

'Too late for me to thank him.' She fell quiet for a moment, remembering. Connor gave her time with her thoughts before he spoke again.

'But you inherited sisters,' he said. 'Tell me more about Eve.'

'She might have held the circumstances of my birth against me at first but we're all good now. She needed closure. I felt honoured to be her bridesmaid last month when she married Nate. And guess what? Eve is an expert horse-woman. The other two ride as well.'

Ana and Connor shared a love of horse-riding. They'd been sent to a horse-riding camp one school holiday when she'd been ten and it had become a passion for both of them. She rode whenever she could. A long-held ambition was to own her own horse. Becoming part-owner of Garrison Downs might help achieve that ambition.

'Did you check out the stables when you were there?'

'Only quickly. There were some magnificent horses. Stud horses for breeding, as well as working horses.'

'I understood those mega cattle-stations mustered using helicopters and motorcycles instead of horses.'

'They do, but apparently Apa was old-fashioned when it came to being on horseback. He rode for pleasure too.'

'That's where you must have got your love of horses from.'

'Is it an inherited thing?'

'Why not, if it's something you have in common with your sisters?'

'I guess so. Rose has taken over Apa's stallion, Jasper. Jasper still grieves the loss of his rider.' She fought the tremor in her voice. 'That day, Rose showed me where…where Apa is buried in the family graveyard.'

'That must have been difficult for you.'

'Yes,' she said, hit by a fresh wave of grief. 'But it was good to hear what had happened from my sisters who were there. Apparently Apa was hit by a falling branch from a gum tree—what they call a "widow maker". He got back on his horse and said he was fine. But then two days later he suddenly collapsed and was taken to hospital by air ambulance. Tilly went with him and Rose stayed for the muster, as Holt would have wanted.'

She paused. 'Rose was in the house when suddenly River, his dog, started to howl. It was eerie and sent shivers down her spine, Rose said. Then the phone rang. It was Tilly telling her their father had just died. River was howling his heartbreak at the loss of his master.' Ana fell silent. It was still unbearable that she'd never had a chance to say goodbye to Apa. She'd been told of his death through a formal communication from Mr Harrington.

'I'm sorry about everything you've had to go through. About River's behaviour—animals just seem to know. There's no explanation for it. And I'm sorry I wasn't there for you.' They walked some more in silence before Connor spoke again. 'Do you have a favourite of your new sisters?'

'That's a tricky one. They're so different. Each sister is so nice in her own way. Tilly, maybe. Though I really like Rose and Eve too. I think everyone loves Tilly. She's warm, open, kind, though she speaks her own mind. You know where you stand with her. Did I tell you she's now a princess? A genuine princess.'

'As distinct from an Outback princess?'

'All three of my sisters are Outback princesses,' Ana said. 'But Tilly is also Princess Matilda of Chaleur. It's a small Mediterranean principality. She's gone back there to be with Henri, her husband. Did I tell you Tilly asked me to make her wedding band for her official royal ceremony in August? I was so thrilled.'

'And you?' said Connor. 'Aren't you an Outback princess now too?'

Ana shook her head. 'I think you have to

be born to it—the Outback, I mean. Besides, I'm from the wrong side of the blanket, as they used to say.'

'Don't put yourself down, Ana.'

She sighed. 'It's true, though. A love child, my mother always calls me, as you know. I don't think I could be an Outback princess even if I wanted to be—more an Outback outsider. Garrison Downs is…daunting. It's like a kingdom. The property in its entirety is probably larger than some small countries. With billionaire Holt as its king and his three beautiful princesses.'

'You're a princess too,' Connor said fiercely. 'Don't you forget that.'

'More Cinderella, really. It's what I feel like.'

'Not so. Your dad recognised you as an equal daughter when it came to inheritance. Step up to it, girl. You're an equal heir to the kingdom. Don't let anyone think any different, especially not you.'

'A red dust kingdom. Remind me not to wear white sneakers the next time I go there.' She paused. 'It's magnificent, Garrison Downs; you should see it.'

'I hope I will one day. I'm counting on an invitation to visit.'

'The second I feel I have the right to invite a guest, the invitation will be yours,' she said.

'I've already picked out a good-looking gelding named Zircon for you to ride. I've fallen for a sweet mare, Ruby. The horses are all named after gemstones. Some whim of my father, apparently.'

'When I heard your news, I looked up everything I could about the property,' Connor said. 'I found pictures of your father's study where he met with visiting statesmen, the ballroom where they hold charity events, endless shots of enormous herds of cattle. By the way, the station is known for its high standard of animal welfare, I'm sure you'll be pleased to know. But there wasn't much about how the family live.'

'In the utmost comfort, I can assure you. There are two fabulous houses and a tiny old settler's cottage going back to the very early days of the property. What they call the old house is the beautiful heritage house where Apa grew up with his parents.'

'And the other house?'

'A mansion. That's the kingdom's castle. Extravagant. Over the top. Like out of a designer magazine. When I stayed there after the reading of the will, Rose put me in the yellow suite. It's like something out of a very posh English country house—or what I imagine one to be. Air-conditioned to the hilt, of course, and run by a housekeeper and staff. Apa had the new house built for his wife Rosamund when he went back to her.'

'To make up for his cheating?'

'Could be. That's not something I could very well ask. The new house is modern—or modern for twenty-five years ago—but timelessly elegant. Rose told me it has her mother Rosamund's stamp all over it. There's an indoor swimming pool because their mum liked to swim. And it's surrounded by beautiful gardens that were their mum's passion too.'

'A garden in the red Outback? They must have good water supplies.'

She smiled. 'Trust you to think of that—always practical. Apparently, there's no shortage of water. In fact, there's a river nearby, but I didn't see that. There's so much I haven't seen.'

Connor stopped walking and turned to face her. He looked into her eyes in that searching way he had. 'It's your heritage, Ana. You need to get to know Garrison Downs. How it works. Where you want your place to be there. Let the others hear your voice. Claim it as your own, equally with your sisters.'

Ana nodded. 'And yet it seems to have been Rosamund's domain. Where does her husband's secret love-child fit in there?'

'Where she makes her place, with the help of her sisters.'

Connor made no mention of the fact there would be no place for Ana to take at Garrison Downs if she wasn't married within six months. Her sisters wouldn't be living there either. The despised descendants of the original owners would be draining the pool and trashing the gardens—or so Rose predicted.

'Wasn't the wife English?' Connor said.

'Half-English, half-French, Tilly says. Apparently it was a terrible shock for a sophisticated, cultured woman to find herself isolated in the heat and the dust of the Outback. No amount of Waverly money could make up for it.'

'It must be strange for you to be immersed in stories about Rosamund Waverly and her influence. She was the rival for your father's affections—Rosamund won, Lili lost.'

Ana shook her head. 'Mum never thought of it that way. Rosamund was his wife, the mother of his three children. If he wanted to make a go of his marriage, my mother thought it was the right—the moral—thing for him to do. Even if she was left heartbroken when he went back. She believed his marriage to be dead; turned out it wasn't. You know I loved my father, but he was far from perfect.'

'You've come to terms with that?'

'A long time ago. Right about the time when I realised I was the only girl in that awful private girls' school who never had a father turn up for school events. Not once. The divorced fathers came but never mine. He couldn't risk his family finding out about me.'

'I remember. So you told them your father was dead.'

'It seemed easier that way. And now...and now he really is dead.'

She sniffed back sudden tears. Cleared her throat. She couldn't give in to that grief now, not in public. 'You've distracted me by talking about my sisters. Before we talk any more about me, there's something I need to say to you.'

'Fire away,' he said. His wary eyes told her he'd been expecting this.

'I'm really sorry we fell out over Brandi. You were right to tell me to butt out of your love life. It wasn't my place.'

A muscle tightened at the corner of his mouth. 'Nothing to forgive. You were right. Turned out she was, shall we say, overly interested in my bank balance.'

'Not your handsome face and charming personality?'

'I think my fat wallet was more appealing. I didn't see it at first. But she got greedy.' There was an edge to Connor's voice.

After Connor had dropped out of medicine he, two other clever guys and a genius girl had formed what they called The Money Club. They'd each wanted their own wealth so they'd be able to take charge of their lives, be independent of their families. The four of them had traded crypto-currency at exactly the right time. They'd invented of-the-moment apps and sold them to the highest bidder. They'd invested in property with perfect timing before a huge boom in prices. The more money they'd made, the more they'd invested and the more they'd made.

The club continued to this day, although the four founding members were now scattered around the world. Connor was a very wealthy guy. With the money to do anything he wanted, he'd decided to go back to uni. Now he'd graduated as a vet. He'd spent much of the past year volunteering on a project working to improve the health of an endangered colony of koalas.

'You really liked Brandi, didn't you?' Ana said.

He hesitated and she wondered if he would brave it out. Connor didn't do vulnerability. 'Yeah. I did. I liked her a lot. I even didn't shut her down when she started to hint about moving in together.'

'That was serious for you.' Connor was notoriously anti-marriage, anti-commitment. His parents' nasty divorce when he'd been a teenager had traumatised him.

'Turned out she wasn't the person she said she was. I should have listened to you and spared myself some drama.'

'When have you ever done that? You hate anyone telling you what to do. Which is why we didn't speak for weeks. We can't let that happen again.'

'Sorry about that. I really am. Even the mention of your name caused a screaming match.' He shuddered. 'But it's over now. I don't want to talk about it.' When Connor broke up with a girlfriend, that was it. A clean break. No keeping in touch. Her number deleted from his phone.

'Maybe you should talk about it,' she said gently. 'Spill the details. Cry on my shoulder. Work it through. You know I'm here for you.'

'And I appreciate that, as always. But there's no point. Brandi is in the past. Right now, I'd rather hear about the hits and misses of your campaign to find a husband.'

'All misses, no hits, I'm afraid.'

'The guys you're meeting must be both blind and stupid.'

She smiled. 'Thank you, friend. It's been quite a hit to the ego, that's for sure.'

'Let's head for the pub. We can talk over a beer about how I can help you. There must be something you could do better. You've only got six months. That's probably not even time to organise a wedding, let alone find the husband to front up to it.'

CHAPTER THREE

CONNOR WAS USED to other guys looking at Ana when he was out with his beautiful friend. Tonight was no different. There'd been admiring, appraising glances from the moment he'd walked through the door of his favourite pub, with Ana sashaying in beside him. She had a subtle but sensual swing of her hips that was pure Ana. He knew she was still fired with the rhythm of their impromptu dance. With her lovely face, slim figure and dazzling smile, she turned heads.

You're a lucky guy. He could read that in the pub patrons' gazes. And he was lucky to have had Ana as his best friend since they'd been little kids.

She'd been five and he seven when the cute little girl next door with her hair in pigtails and a scattering of freckles across her nose had burrowed her way through a gap in the dividing hedge and fallen into his back yard. He and his brother Billy, who had been playing there at the time, hadn't known what to make of her. But little Ana had joined in every rough and tumble game with him and his brother, who was three years younger than he was. She was a whiz at cricket. Swam like a fish. Her slight, slender frame made her good at gymnastics.

His parents had expected that Ana would play more with Billy, who was closer to her age. But there'd been a bond between Connor and Ana from the word go. Almost, he thought, from the moment he'd picked leaves and sticks from the hedge out of her hair. He'd always felt protective of her and she of him—not that he'd needed protecting, especially by a girl.

When she'd been fifteen, she'd gone on holiday to Budapest with her mother and grandparents. He'd missed her. But, when she'd come back, she'd seemed different. It had taken a while for him to get used to a new, more *girly* Ana. She'd dressed differently and had found an interest in jewellery, having spent time with a great-uncle who was a jeweller of some repute. Connor's guy friends had started to take an interest in his lovely, very feminine neighbour.

Yet he had always been determined to keep their friendship just that. Ana was out of bounds as far as dating went. Never spoken of, but never forgotten, was the kiss they'd shared when he'd escorted her—as a friend—to her school formal. He'd suspected it was her first proper kiss but it had sizzled—the heat of it totally taking him by surprise. But he was two years older than she was. She'd been too young for the kind of kiss that had screamed 'going exclusive'. He wasn't ready for that, and she certainly hadn't been either—no matter what she might have thought.

He'd known stepping out of the friendship zone could be a risk, and back then he hadn't been able to bear the thought of losing he. Not at a time of immense change for him with the disintegration of his parents' marriage. Teen-aged Connor had clung to Ana for support and reassurance during the time when his mother had discovered his father had cheated on her throughout their marriage. Ana's friendship had given him stability at a time when he couldn't have dealt with more change. She'd been the only person he'd been able to confide in about what was going on. Ana was accustomed to keeping secrets. Even today, he felt she was the only person he could truly be himself with.

Now he sat opposite Ana in the privacy of a corner booth. She was looking particularly lovely tonight, with her black hair tied back in a high pony-tail, her cheeks flushed pink from dancing, her astounding blue eyes defined with dark make-up. Who'd have known those eyes would bond her to her newly found half-sisters?

He'd wondered if the three Waverly girls would insist on a DNA test when Ana had appeared, seemingly from nowhere, as a claimant to the will. But it seemed her father's acknowledgement of a fourth daughter and the Waverly eyes had been enough. Still, he'd warned her to be careful about giving too much of herself until she knew for sure that the sisterly love was genuine. Not that she seemed to want to listen to that particular piece of advice. She was enchanted by her new sisters.

'Okay, spill,' he said. 'Tell me all about the husband hunt.'

Over the background chatter and clinking of glasses, he listened with increasing incredulity as Ana regaled him with tales of her desperately bad dates. The condescending creeps. The guys who had obviously lopped off twenty years from their real ages for the dating apps. The seriously weird and the just plain boring. Then there had been the guys who'd thought insults were a form of flirtation.

He heard about her grandmother's well-meaning attempts to find her a suitable husband. And her dread of reporting to her sisters how she was no closer to finding the all-important man—or woman, for that matter. It didn't state in the will that it couldn't be a same-sex marriage, but he knew Ana didn't swing that way. He hated seeing her so anxious about a clause in a will that was so archaic and constricting. Ana had always been slim, but she'd lost weight. There were bruise-like shadows under her eyes and a frailty about her that he found alarming.

Finally, he put up his hand in a halt sign. 'Stop! You're going about this in entirely the wrong way.'

Her eyes widened. She stopped mid-word. 'What do you mean?'

'Seems to me you're preparing to throw your life away for the sake of your inheritance.'

'You mean by getting married? Of course I wasn't planning to get married just yet but—'

'I mean by forcing a marriage. The condition in the will says all four of you have to be married within a year, right? Otherwise, bye-bye Garrison Downs, the source of much of the Waverly wealth.'

'And the beloved home of my sisters,' she reminded him.

'Where does it say in the will that it has to be a real marriage?' he said.

Ana paused. Only because he'd known her for so long was he able to get a clue about her feelings from reading her face. She'd had to keep so much secret for so long, she'd mastered the art of masking her emotions. Now he saw confusion. 'Um. Nowhere, to my knowledge.'

'Or does it state somewhere that it has to be a lasting marriage? Or, indeed, a love match?'

She frowned. 'Nowhere.'

'Or that it has to be a consummated marriage?'

Ana flushed, which told him she was thinking what he was thinking about consummation. Only in his thoughts he was with her, not she with some stranger she'd married. He forced thoughts of *that* from his mind—as he'd been doing for years. He had never allowed himself to think of Ana in a non-platonic way. That hadn't always easy. But staying just friends worked best for him.

'It…it certainly doesn't say anything about… about consummating the marriage anywhere in the document,' she said.

Connor sat back in the booth. 'So why are you running around trying to find happy-ever-after love to fit some artificial deadline? You can't force it. No wonder you seem so tense and anxious when you talk about it.'

'I am not tense and anxious.'

He stared pointedly at her hands, which she was wringing together so tightly, he could hardly tell which fingers belonged to which hand.

'Okay. Maybe a bit tense and anxious. Actually, more than a bit.'

'No wonder. Even if you find a guy you think you could spend your life with, what kind of pressure would be on him? On both of you? Have you thought past the wedding to sharing a life together?'

Her mouth turned downwards. 'I haven't met anyone who I'd imagine spending a weekend with, let alone my life.'

'So why do that?' He leaned across the table, closer to her. 'Look at this marriage thing as a business proposal. Instead of trying to force happy-ever-afters, find someone who you can marry to fulfil the terms of the will. Pay him a substantial fee. Then quietly divorce after the inheritance is settled on all four sisters.'

His friend was so smart, he wondered why she hadn't thought of this, or her sisters.

She frowned. 'You mean, hire a husband?'

'I wouldn't put it quite like that, but yes.'

'Bizarre idea, but…' He could see the cogs turning. 'How would it work?'

'You'd draw up a contract for his services to be your husband, in name only, for a year, starting with a fake engagement, leading to a wedding and then a discreet divorce.'

'A fake marriage?'

'It would have to be a legal marriage before

a celebrant to satisfy the terms of the will. You couldn't risk it unravelling if it was found to be fraudulent. But it wouldn't be fraudulent if the marriage didn't work out and you separated soon after.'

She nodded thoughtfully. 'I think, under Australian law, you have to be separated for a year before you can file for divorce.'

'All that would mean is you couldn't marry anyone else for at least a year.'

She shrugged. 'As I don't want to get married at all, that wouldn't be a hardship.'

He wasn't sure why she was so vehemently against marriage. It might date back to the awful guy, Rory, the longest-lasting of her boyfriends. He'd been a manipulative bully. Connor had seen that, but it had taken Ana a while to wake up to it.

He was no fan of marriage either. Especially after his experience with Brandi. He'd had a close escape. How viciously she'd turned on him when she'd realised he'd seen through her. Everything he'd thought had been spontaneous about her had been calculating. He could only imagine how much worse it would have got if he'd stayed.

'The guy you choose to sign up to the contract would have to be a good actor,' he said.

'And attractive enough for it to be believable that you would fall for him so quickly.'

'Someone I wouldn't have trouble pretending to fancy. But…it would be a marriage in name only.' She grimaced. 'No sex. There couldn't be sex.'

'Not if you didn't want it.'

'I wouldn't sleep with some guy just to—'

'Inherit millions of dollars? Of course you wouldn't. Some might. But I know you would never contemplate that.'

He couldn't help a grin. She smiled back. 'How would I go about it?' she asked.

'A water-tight contract. Confidentiality clause. And a hefty fee. The inheritance will make you a very wealthy woman. You can afford to pay top dollar to make it worth your potential candidate's while. Borrow against your house if you have to. The pay-off from your inheritance would be worth it.'

'Where would I find such a candidate?' she said.

'You're considering it?' He was surprised, as Ana was usually pretty much a go-by-the-rules person.

'It's kinda out there,' she admitted. 'But I suppose it could work. I'm open to all ideas to allow me to get that inheritance. Not just for me but for my sisters.'

'Good,' he said.

'But where would I find this…this fake husband?'

'Let me think,' Connor said. 'Your guy would have to be good-looking and a good actor. So why not an actual actor?'

'That's a thought,' she said slowly. 'Not that I know any actors.'

'Actors have agents,' he said.

Her eyes narrowed. 'But could you go through an agent with such an unconventional role? I doubt they'd let me through the door. It would also mean another person I'd have to let in on the secret.'

'Good point. The fewer people who know about the hire-a-husband contract, the better.'

'Understood,' she said.

'Were there any actors on the dating apps?' Connor asked.

'You mean the genuine kind, as opposed to the ones who were pretending to be someone they weren't?' she said. 'I thought I recognised two. I wondered at the time why they would put themselves out there on an app.'

'Genuinely looking for connection, I suggest. Finding a compatible partner isn't easy for anyone. I reckon some celebrities could have problems being appreciated for their genuine selves.' He knew now to be concerned that someone—a person like Brandi—could be with him for his wealth. It had been kick-in-the-gut hurtful to find out the truth about the woman he'd been infatuated with.

Ana's finely winged eyebrows rose in alarm. 'That might be so. But I can't have a celebrity. The fake husband couldn't be someone well-known. That would totally attract the wrong kind of attention to the wedding.'

He nodded. 'A struggling, unknown actor might be the best candidate.'

She sighed. 'It's a good idea. But I'd have to be so, so careful. How on earth could I put that kind of trust in a stranger? They could break the contract and go to press with the truth of a fake marriage. The repercussions of being exposed don't bear thinking about.'

'True. There's a lot at stake.'

'Not just for me, but for my sisters.'

He thought about it but came to a dead-end every time. 'What about someone you actually know?'

She paused. 'There is someone. Maybe. One of my grandmother's matchmaking efforts. He's gorgeous, fun and hiding the fact he's gay from his family. I liked him a lot and we've agreed to stay in touch. He's establishing his own business, so might welcome the money.'

'Could be worth considering.'

It was strange but all this talk of Ana getting married was stirring up some unfamiliar emotions—the most insistent one being jealousy. One day, each of them would most likely get married. Even him, although that seemed the remotest of remote possibilities right now. It would be lucky if they each married someone who tolerated their spouse having a straight best friend of the opposite sex. Brandi had hated him having contact with Ana. Ana had only had a few serious boyfriends. They hadn't exactly encouraged her to spend time with Connor. One of them had been outright hostile. But he couldn't be jealous of a hire-a-husband. He couldn't be jealous of anyone. Ana was just a friend. That didn't stop him from wanting to protect her, though, as he always had.

'Wait, now that I think of it, that won't work,' said Ana. 'My new friend has a partner. He wants to get married as soon as they can, once he comes clean to his family about his sexuality. They wouldn't welcome not being able to marry for more than a year because he was legally tied to me.'

'Shame. Count him out, then,' Connor said. 'But you've only just started thinking about this alternative marriage possibility. There must be other possibilities—an anonymous advertisement on the Internet could be an idea.'

Ana vehemently shook her head. 'I can tell you right now, I wouldn't do that. Way too risky.'

'You're right,' he said. 'Of course you are.'

'I'll ask Kartika if she has any thoughts,' Ana said.

Kartika was Ana's best female friend and a really nice person. Ana had met her at university. Kartika was Indonesian and now lived back in Jakarta, working in her wealthy family's business. She was also Ana's partner in their online jewellery store and was as keen as Ana was to expand it.

'Is that wise?' he said. 'Bringing another person into your confidence?'

'I trust Kartika implicitly. If I went ahead with this crazy scheme, only you and she would know anything about it.'

'If you say so.' Connor drained the last of his beer. 'We've got a ticking clock against us. We really need to put our thinking caps on, as my grandmother used to say. I'll go get us more drinks and then we can get a recruitment plan into action.'

Ana sighed. 'Or we can forget all about what is a completely off-the-wall idea.'

'That too,' he said. He still felt uneasy at the thought of Ana actually marrying a stranger. What if he became abusive? Tried to scam her? Or what if she chose someone so compatible it actually became a real marriage? He wasn't at all sure that was a good idea.

There was a queue at the bar. When Connor eventually got back to the table, it was to find Ana scrolling through her phone. She looked up, eyes alight.

'What you propose is called a "marriage of convenience". It's more common than you might think, when oddly worded wills that specify marriage are in play.' She smiled. 'And apparently popular in romance novels.'

'Really? I'm more than a bit miffed to find it wasn't a brilliant original idea of mine,' he said lightly.

As he pushed Ana's glass of wine towards her, Connor was surprised to see how animated she was—excited, it seemed, about a possible marriage of convenience.

'So you think my idea is a feasible one?' he said, more than a little chuffed that she should think so. And more than a little concerned about the possibility of her marrying a stranger.

'The more I think about it, the more I think it could be an excellent solution to an impossible problem.' She took a sip from her wine and looked across at him, head tilted to one side, very serious. 'I've even thought of the perfect man to be my pretend husband. He fits every criterion we discussed. He is absolutely the one. There could be no other choice.'

'And who might that be?' Connor asked.

Ana put down her glass and moved closer to him across the table. 'You.'

CHAPTER FOUR

ANA WATCHED IN alarm as Connor nearly choked on his beer, spluttering and gasping for air. She slid round in the booth so she could pat him vigorously on his back. Finally, he got his breath back.

'Me? Are you serious?' he choked out.

'Very serious,' she said. 'I don't know why I didn't think of it straight away. You would be perfect as my pretend husband.'

'Perfect? Me?' His green eyes glazed with disbelief. 'What makes you say that?'

Ana wasn't sure whether to be offended or amused that Connor appeared so shocked at her proposal. *Proposal.* There was a proposal in a business context, or a proposal in the context of asking someone to marry you. This was, she supposed, neither one nor the other.

'The fake marriage was your idea. You'd be able to carry it through better than anyone. When I thought about it, I realised you so perfectly fit all the criteria we discussed.'

Her friend shook his head, obviously be-wildered. 'You know I'm usually not lost for words, but I... I don't know what to say.'

Ana could see he wasn't just shocked. Con-nor was obviously appalled and horrified. She was mortified. His reaction shot her right back to the time she'd so foolishly suggested they lose their virginities together. She'd gone too far. Taken too much for granted. Totally ru-ined their reunion after six months apart. She shuffled back from where she sat next to him to her place opposite in the booth. She wished she could shuffle right out of the pub.

Her cheeks burned with humiliation. She could hardly bear to look at him. Frantically, she tried to back-pedal. 'Of course it's a terri-ble idea. I'm sorry. Forget I mentioned it. Silly of me.' She attempted a carefree laugh, but it came out as a strangled, hysterical squeak. She looked down at her watch and faked surprise at seeing the time. 'Anyway, I think I need to go.' She went to get up. How could she ever live down this fiasco?

'No. Stay.' Connor reached over the table to put his hand on her arm to stop her. 'I was sur-prised, that's all. You know I'm not the marry-ing kind. Just a mention of the word gives me shivers of aversion. And I don't like lies or dis-honesty. We talked about acting skills, but really it would be lying and deception on a grand scale that would be required.'

'I should have known better than to even suggest it.' Ana squeezed shut her eyes, wishing that when she opened them she could be anywhere but here. When she did open them, it was to see Connor, no longer horrified but concerned. Compassion and understanding warmed his eyes. He knew her so well.

'Quite rightly, you felt you could ask me,' he said. 'We're friends. We help each other out. I've always looked out for you. You need help now. It's just—'

'I know,' she said, wanting to extricate herself from the confines of the booth, feeling edgy with embarrassment.

'No, you don't know. You're jumping to conclusions. You shocked me. Now I've got over my shock, I want to hear what you have to say. Run me through those criteria again.'

'You'll just laugh,' she said, knowing she sounded a little sulky, unable to help it.

'I won't. Well, I might laugh at the ridiculousness of me being anyone's husband, even a pretend one. But I wouldn't be laughing at you. Never would I laugh at you.'

There was an edge to his voice that made Ana put her embarrassment aside and focus on Connor. He'd just gone through a bitter breakup. She knew he feared he could never be faithful to a woman. That was why marriage—a real marriage—was something he didn't think he could succeed at. He'd grown up being told he was just like his handsome but unfaithful father in terms of looks, brains and personality. Then the image of his father had been shattered and so, in some way, had his image of himself. She hadn't realised it went quite so deep.

'You know that's not true,' she said. 'When you find the right person, you'll be a wonderful husband. You're a more honourable and loyal person than your father in every way. I really believe that.'

Connor's mouth twisted wryly. 'You know I'd like to believe you, but I'm not so sure I'll ever want to marry for real. So tell me why I'd make a good fake husband.'

'Are you sure you want to hear me out?'

'Absolutely sure. I'm not saying I'll say yes. I just want to hear your rationale for my fitness for the role.'

'I don't expect you to say yes. Well, obviously I was hoping you might say yes, or I wouldn't have suggested it. But in light of your spontaneous adverse reaction, I've completely revised that expectation. Weighing up the probability, I—'

'I love it when you talk like an accountant.'

He was smiling at her, that gorgeous Connor smile that she had never been able to resist. She couldn't resist it this time either. She smiled back. Then they were laughing together, as they had done so many times before. This was Connor. Her best friend. She had completely overreacted. The husband-hunting thing had her on edge.

'The criteria?' he prompted. 'And please don't ask me again if I'm sure.'

'Okay,' she said, relaxing back into the booth, happy they'd got over the awkwardness. She couldn't bear it when things weren't good with them. Those months when they hadn't spoken had left their mark. She had missed him every day. 'First, a marriage between us would be believable. We've known each other most of our lives. That woman earlier this evening wasn't the first one to take us for a couple.'

'There have been others, yes. And we've each helped the other out when in need of a date. We would be believable.'

'We know each other so well, we wouldn't trip ourselves up with details of our lives that would make people suspicious we weren't for real.'

'True.'

'There are other reasons you'd be ideal. You're not in a relationship, you're in no hurry to actually get married and you're so ridiculously rich you wouldn't try to blackmail me to cash in on the inheritance.'

'Correct on all counts,' he said. 'But I—'

Ana put up her hand in a halt signal. 'Can we save the objections to the end? You know how difficult this is for me. Let's face it, employing a fake husband is tantamount to admitting I can't find a real one.'

'Ana, that's not true. You're everything a guy would want in a wife—beautiful, kind, smart.'

Just what her grandma had said. What about sexy, exciting, adventurous? But Ana knew, up until now, she had trod the safe path. That was her family's influence. They were obsessed with security. She owed them so much. As a good daughter and granddaughter, she'd gone along with what they wanted for her—a degree in finance with a sure job at the end of it. A secure role in a big accountancy firm, where she felt both bored and trapped. The inheritance opened new horizons for her. The freedom to follow her creative impulses. Her own business. Security of a very different kind. And the chance to change.

'Thank you,' she said.

'I meant if a guy was ready to marry. Not like me. You know why I don't have marriage on my radar.'

Ana knew Connor feared his capacity for fidelity because of his father's multiple betrayals. It was why he got out of relationships when talk of commitment came calling. She hoped his experience with dollar-signs-in-her-eyes Brandi wouldn't embitter him.

'I don't want to get married either,' she said. 'I want to fly, Connor, without having to take into consideration someone else's needs. I don't want to be tethered any longer by other people's expectations of me. I've loved studying part-time for my jewellery-design qualifications. It's not just a hobby for me. I want it to be my career. You know that. I want to invest my time and my money in my business with Kartika. I need to be free of obligations so I can travel to where we source the materials and have the jewellery made on a more commercial scale. We need to do marketing and publicity too. The inheritance will give me all that. I can't be tied down by a marriage. Not a real one. Or a fake one with someone I don't trust.'

'Trust has to come into it on both sides,' he said slowly.

'I know I can trust you above anyone else. I know you would play the role convincingly and with sincerity. With you as my fake husband, I know there would be no leaks to the press and no blackmail attempts down the track. I can trust your integrity.'

'You can always trust me. That goes without saying. I know I can trust you. We've kept each other's secrets since we were kids. But this is really serious, Ana. I believe the fake marriage idea is a good one, considering your circumstances. But you and I have so much history, and so much to lose if it didn't work out.'

Connor leaned closer across the table and took both her hands in his. They rarely touched, so Ana could tell how seriously he took her proposal.

'You're going to say no?' she said. She swallowed hard against a lump of disappointment that threatened to choke her.

He looked directly into her face in that way he had. 'I'm going to say I want to think about this. You know I'm always on your side. But something about this "marriage of convenience" proposal scares me. And that's apart from the prospect of lying to our families and friends.'

She frowned. 'Scares you?'

'You know how much I value your friendship. What if we went through with this and it didn't work out? It would be a really big thing to go into, and an equally big thing to come out of. I don't want to risk losing you. You know what I say: girlfriends come and go, but Ana is for ever.'

Ana wondered if he would again say he thought of her as a sister. Because ever since that kiss they'd shared, she'd never thought of him as a brother.

'We'd be aware of that,' she said. 'I wouldn't want to risk losing my friendship with you either. I value it so much.' She tightened her grip on his hands. 'Don't think I would ask this of you if I had any other choice.'

'I'm aware of that,' he said.

'We're both intelligent people; I think we could make it work. Please, Connor, help me out. This was your idea, after all. I can't even contemplate a fake marriage with a stranger. It's too risky and I fear it could backfire on me. Yet I have to marry within six months. It would be so unfair if my sisters missed out on their inheritance because I couldn't find a man. Unfair on me too, because Garrison Downs and the wealth it generates is as much my birth right as it is theirs.'

'Understood,' he said.

'I also want to claim that birth right for my mother, who brought me up pretty much as a single mum. She put her own life on hold for way too long. And for my grandparents, who spent so much time and love on me and were civil about Holt—a man they loathed—for my sake.'

'You make a compelling argument for me to consider,' he said.

Ana realised it was so compelling that, by trying to talk him into the plan, she'd talked herself into it one hundred percent. Now she believed there could be no other way to meet the requirement of the will than to go through with a fake marriage to Connor. Panic gripped her at the thought of him refusing to step up.

But there was one big problem that suddenly blazed into her consciousness. Something she couldn't share with him. If he agreed to her proposal, she would spend way more time with him than she had since they'd been children. They would be thrust into an enforced intimacy. What if she found herself unable to keep up the pretence that she wasn't attracted to him?

Connor realised his hands were still entwined with Ana's across the table. And that they had leaned so closely towards each other, their heads were nearly touching. Just as well. That way, no one could possibly have overheard what they were saying. And they really didn't want this conversation to be overheard.

He gently disengaged their hands and Ana drew back. Her cheeks were flushed pink,

which served to make her eyes seem even bluer.
Tendrils of her dark hair had come loose from
where they'd been pulled back in her ponytail,
and they wisped around her face. Her bold red
lipstick had worn off, but her mouth was naturally pink.

Her mouth. It was a part of Ana that Connor never allowed himself to focus on. Her full
lips were eminently kissable, but he could never
acknowledge that. Back in their teenage days,
when she'd suddenly turned so feminine and
elegant after her trip to Budapest, the boys at
school had certainly noticed. He'd been protective and had refused to facilitate introductions.
He'd guarded her.

'If you don't want her, mate, don't hog her to
yourself,' the boys had said.

He'd growled back that they weren't good
enough for her.

He had wanted her. But she'd been too young
and he hadn't been ready. A two-year age gap
had loomed large in those days. And then everything had fallen apart with his family. His
father had moved out and he'd stayed in the
family home at St Kilda with his mother. Next
door to Ana. He'd been happy for her to remain
the girl next-door who offered uncomplicated
friendship. He'd needed that so badly. From
then on, they'd stayed firmly in the friendship

zone. She'd lost her virginity to someone else—her first serious boyfriend at uni, most likely. He hadn't asked, hadn't wanted to know, still didn't want to know.

'How long do you need to think before you can make a decision?' she asked.

Ana had offered him friendship and comfort when he'd really needed it. She'd been a loyal friend in the intervening years. Now was the time to return the favour.

She needed him.

'I've had enough time,' he said.

'Really?'

'I've made a decision.'

Her eyes widened. 'And?'

'Ana Horvath, will you marry me?' he said.

'*What?*'

'I'm stepping into the role straight away. I realise I'm a traditional kind of guy when it comes to marriage, even of the fake kind. I want to do the proposing.'

'Oh, Connor. Thank you. I… I'm so grateful. So grateful I could kiss you.' She stopped. 'Should I kiss you?'

For a long moment, their gazes met, full of unspoken questions. *Yes!* he wanted to say. But that would complicate this raw, new agreement between them.

'Not now,' he said, finding it remarkably difficult to utter those two words. Suddenly all he could think about was kissing her. He tried very hard to avert his eyes from her mouth. 'You'll have to kiss me at some stage soon if we're to make a relationship believable and authentic. We'll have to sort out how we handle the...uh... public displays of affection.'

'Yes. We will. PDAs to be choreographed.' She looked down at the table, unable to meet his gaze. Did she feel any of the same pull to him? Or was he just a convenient solution to her problem? 'But we're both private people,' she said. 'We can probably keep the PDAs to a minimum. No one we know would expect us to...to be all over each other.'

He cleared his throat. 'Perhaps not.'

Ana all over him? Now that was a thought.

She looked up again. 'We'll figure it out.'

'But, in the meantime, are you accepting my proposal or not?' he said.

'Yes, I am,' she said. Connor saw the worry lift from her face to be replaced by relief. That made it worthwhile. She laughed. 'I can't believe we're doing this!'

'Consider ourselves engaged,' he said. Never would he have imagined himself saying those words. Ironic that it was just a game.

'That seems kinda weird, doesn't it?' she said, her head tilted to one side.

'If I was a real fiancé, I'd be affronted you said that. But, as I'm a fake, I'd have to agree. Yes. Seriously weird.'

'But I'm so grateful.'

'And I'm so glad I can be of help.'

'What's next?' she said.

Connor didn't have to think hard. 'We tell the right people that we're getting married.'

'Who first?' she asked.

'Your sisters. Face to face, with a visit to Garrison Downs. Then your family. Then mine. Billy, of course. He'll be gutted. He's had a secret crush on you for years.'

Her eyebrows rose. 'Your little brother, Billy?'

'Not so little now. He's only a year younger than you are. He can be my best man.'

'Best man? Oh, my gosh, we'll have to have a wedding, won't we? A proper wedding. I hadn't thought of that.'

'We haven't had time to think about a lot of things,' he said. 'But surprise engagements are like that.'

'You're right into the play-acting already,' she said, smiling. 'I'm impressed.'

'If we don't get deep into it straight away, we might have trouble ahead of us,' he said. 'From now on, you have to seriously believe you're engaged to me. I won't be the only one acting. Do you think you're up to it?'

'Of course I am,' she said. 'If you remember, I took part in a few university revues.'

'Indeed you did, but you didn't invite me,' he said.

'I was a bit too self-conscious,' she admitted. 'But I think the experience will help me play the role of besotted bride.'

He frowned. 'Besotted?'

'Come on, Connor. Have you ever had a girl-friend who wasn't besotted with you?'

'I wouldn't say *besotted*...'

'You're very handsome, clever, a decent human being and very, very wealthy. I would definitely say besotted. If I—'

'If you what?' he said.

'Nothing,' she said, casting down her gaze again.

'You can't say *nothing*. Come on.'

She looked up. Her cheeks flushed a deeper shade of pink. 'If I were seriously dating you, and wasn't your friend who's known you since you were a grubby little boy, I... I would be besotted.' She paused. 'That's not to say I *am* besotted, you understand. I'm talking about a hypothetical situation.'

'Hypothetical. Of course.' Just the same, he couldn't help but feel pleased. Because wasn't it the truth that she'd always been special to him, even when he'd been a little boy? 'Hypothetically speaking, if I wasn't the boy who had to wipe up your bloodied knees every time you crashed my skateboard—'

'If I recall, it was one of your doctor parents who tended to my bloodied knees. And I only crashed your skateboard because you dared me to go too fast. You kept on daring me.'

'And you kept on crashing my skateboard.'

'Until the day I got my own skateboard.'

'And we went down that hill side by side.'

'Yes,' she said, smiling. 'Really fast.'

How innocent those days had been, with both his parents living together at home and available to patch up knees and elbows or put stitches in a gashed forehead. Without thinking about it, he put his hand up to his head. He still had the scar, faded now, just below his hairline. The scars caused by his parents' divorce went so much deeper.

'So…you were saying?' Ana asked. 'Hypothetically, that is?'

'Hypothetically, I'd be besotted with you.'

'Really?'

'Like most of the neighbourhood boys were. But you didn't even notice.'

'Don't be silly, of course they weren't. They were interested in tall, tanned, leggy blondes.'

'Not all of them. Some were very keen on you. Don't worry, I fought them off for you.'

'You *what*?'

'I didn't think they were worthy of you.'

'Like I didn't think Brandi was worthy of you.'

'Touché,' he said.

She laughed. 'I don't remember those boys very well. I would, if any of them had interested me. Also, if you remember, my grandparents and mother were really strict with me. After all, my mother had got pregnant to a married man at age twenty-five. They were going to make darn sure that no such unplanned pregnancy happened to me. They loved it when we took up horse-riding because it was ninety-five percent girls at the horse camps.'

'Me being the five percent boy.'

'That's right. The girls made such a fuss of you.'

'And I stuck with my friend, Ana,' he said. 'It wasn't a hardship. You're very lovely, you know. And you were very cute when you were a teenager.'

Their eyes met for too long. Hers were the first to drop. 'Nice to reminisce,' she said briskly. 'But that's not progressing our marriage-of-convenience agenda, is it?'

'Spoken like you're chairing a meeting,' he said.

'Which I often do at the office,' she said. 'I can't wait to hand in my resignation.'

'Perhaps you should do that soon. Can you afford to?'

'If I'm careful, yes. But I can't count on the inheritance until all four of us sisters are married. I'm not sure there's anyone on the horizon for Rose. Perhaps we should share our idea with her.'

'Not a good idea,' he said. 'I don't think we should tell anyone the truth. Not your sisters. Not your family. Not Kartika. There's no need to take her into your confidence now that I'm the fake fiancé. You and I can be the only ones to know it's not for real.'

'Understood,' she said. 'Safer that way.' She paused. 'A ring. We'll need an engagement ring.'

'I can buy one.'

'I can make one.'

'Make it blingy,' he said. 'I don't want to be seen as stingy.'

'Blue sapphire and diamonds, I think,' she said. 'Something modern and simple. I can wear it on the other hand after the divorce.' She sobered. 'That also sounds weird. I'll spend the rest of my life as your ex-wife.'

'And me as your ex-husband,' he said. 'But let's make sure we're the kind of exes who stay friends.'

'Absolutely.'

'Do you need me to sub you for the ring?' he said.

'No. I can pay for the gems myself—easier that way.' She paused. 'Do I need to pay you that substantial hire-a-husband fee we talked about? I'd rather not have to mortgage the house.'

The title to her family home in St Kilda had been transferred to her, under the terms of an agreement with her father, when she'd turned twenty-one. It had been a welcome surprise. She had lived there alone since her mother had moved out to live with Ben. One of the bedrooms had been converted to be her jewellery workshop.

'Of course you don't,' he said. 'I don't know why you asked.'

'I didn't think so. It's not as if you need the money. But I had to check to be sure. We have to be spot on with our communication.'

'Let's agree that, if there's something one of us is not sure of, we keep quiet until we can discuss it with the other.'

'Understood.' She sighed. 'I can't tell you how relieved I am that I can stop the husband hunt. It was awful. Thank you. Thank you, *darling*,' she said, then ruined the effect with a peal of giggles. 'Did you like that?'

He rolled his eyes. 'Darling. Sweetheart. Honey. You decide. I'd rather just be Connor.'

'I quite like *my love*,' she said.

'I'd still prefer Connor,' he replied, more abruptly than he'd intended. 'Nothing personal, I just find such terms insincere.' All the time he'd been cheating on her, his father had called his wife 'honey'. Total hypocrisy. He shifted in his seat. Time to change the subject.

'You said once you could read my mind. You failed dismally. Do you want to try again?'

Her brow furrowed. 'Okay.'

'What am I thinking right now?' he challenged her.

She narrowed her eyes almost to slits as she perused his face. Then her eyes widened. 'No, Connor. You couldn't be.'

'Couldn't be what?'

'You couldn't be hungry. Not after the *gulyas* and the strudel that followed.'

'That was a few hours ago. Of course I'm hungry.' He paused. 'How did you guess so quickly?'

She knew him so well.

'Years of observation,' she said dryly. 'You didn't exactly look deep in philosophical thought.'

He laughed. 'The burgers are good in this pub. While we're here, we might as well order one.'

'You can. I'm not in the slightest bit hungry.

Besides, as you know, I don't care for fast food. You remember the way I was brought up—only home cooking will do.'

'You know the way I was brought up—your classic latchkey kid. Parents running a busy general practice. Often with out-of-hours emergencies. Never on top of their paperwork. For medical practitioners, they knew surprisingly little about nutrition when it came to feeding two hungry boys. Burgers, pizza, and fish and chips featured often on the menu.'

'Fortunately for you, and Billy too, the girl-next-door's grandparents ran a restaurant not far from our homes.'

'Very fortunately for me. But I did acquire the taste for a good burger. And I want one now. Are you sure I can't order one for you? Last chance.'

'I'll just nibble on a few of your chips,' she said.

'Spoken like a true fiancée,' he said, laughing.

'Let's have fun with this fake marriage,' she said. She leaned across and took his hand. She stroked the palm with her slender fingers. 'First PDA,' she said, with a husky, sensual voice he'd never heard from her. She looked into his eyes and pouted with her lush mouth. 'How am I doing?'

'Well,' he said. He cleared his throat. 'Uh… very well.'

Too well.

Because he was getting aroused. By Ana. That couldn't be, even if she was his fake fiancée. *Especially* because she was his fake fiancée.

CHAPTER FIVE

TEN DAYS LATER, Ana peered out of the window of the two-seater private plane piloted by Connor, taking them to Garrison Downs for the weekend. They'd been flying over endless tracts of red dirt punctuated by hummocks of spinifex grass, coarse scrub and stunted trees. This was truly the Australian outback: harsh, unrelenting, with its own wild beauty. She noticed a small mob of kangaroos bounding along the bed of a dried-up creek.

Suddenly there were signs they were nearing their destination: more vegetation, fencing, pastures, vast herds of cattle, cattle yards and a river surrounded by rocky outcrops. Then she recognised the buildings at the heart of the kingdom surrounded by an oasis of green as Connor circled, preparing to land.

She snapped a few photos with her phone to show her family. She could, she supposed, caption the photos as 'my new home'. But could she ever shake off the feeling that this place was, in fact, home to her father's *other* family— what she still could not help thinking of as his *real* family? Who had used that phrase during her childhood? Her mother? Her grandfather? It had stuck.

She and Connor were wearing headphones and microphones so they could communicate over the sound of the twin-engine plane. Right now, he was getting landing instructions from Rose. Connor was so competent, sure of himself, and she had utter confidence in him. He'd got his recreational pilot's licence while he'd still been at university. When he'd suggested the private plane, rather than commercial flights and long drives, she'd jumped at it. They'd set off from Melbourne's Moorabbin Airport.

Was there anything Connor couldn't succeed at? He could pilot a plane, perform surgery on animals and make money on a large scale. He really was an excellent choice for a fake fiancé. She knew her sisters would be impressed. His practical skills and knowledge would be valued out here.

And that was on top of his personal charm.

Connor was the kind of person people naturally gravitated towards. Who would blame them? She'd spotted how attractive he was when she'd been five years old and had dived through that hedge. She still remembered how she'd wanted to play with that boy and nothing had been going to stop her. What would it be like to play with him now—that boy all grown up? That man, now her fake fiancé? She felt a little shiver of desire at the thought. There was too much at risk for her to allow her thoughts to stray that way. Nothing had changed between them. They were still just friends.

'That, below, is what it's all about,' Connor said. 'Your birth right. How are you feeling about it all, now we're so close?'

'To be honest? Anxious and a tad overwhelmed,' she admitted. 'It was all very well planning our fake engagement in Melbourne but, actually being out here, I realise it's such a big deal. I feel enough of an imposter as it is.'

'You are not an imposter. Your father's will says four daughters will own this place, not three. Keep that in mind. You're doing your best to play your part in securing it for all of you.'

'So are you,' she said. 'I'll always be grateful for that.'

'Don't worry, I'll think of ways you can pay me back for years to come,' he said, smiling.

'I'm sure you will,' she replied, also smiling. She refused to let her thoughts run to exciting ways that payback could happen. Because he had made it very clear he simply didn't see her as anything other than a close friend. 'Look, more kangaroos,' she pointed out, glad for the distraction.

In spite of Connor's reassuring words, Ana realised she was twisting the engagement ring round and round on the third finger of her left hand. She hadn't created a ring for herself in her workshop back in St Kilda after all. She hadn't had time—or, truth be told, the inclination. Connor was right: they needed attention-grabbing bling to shout out her engagement to a very wealthy man, not the discreetly elegant sapphire ring she'd want if she were really getting engaged. This needed to be a megaphone of a ring.

She'd contacted a friend from her jewellery design course and purchased wholesale a gorgeous four-carat, emerald-cut diamond solitaire, with small diamonds studded all around the band. It was as big a diamond as her slender hand could take. When she'd shown it to Connor, he'd stared. 'Can you afford that? You have to let me pay for it,' he'd said.

Ana had laughed. 'Impressive, isn't it? They're laboratory-made diamonds, not mined diamonds, so it's pricey, but not horrendously so.'

'I can't tell the difference,' Connor had said.

'Not many people can,' she'd said. 'Fake diamonds for a fake engagement. Appropriate, I thought.'

'And yet the diamonds appear to be real.'

Just like their relationship would have to appear.

'If anyone asks, let's say we chose the ring together,' she had said.

In the days before they'd left Melbourne, she and Connor had spent time getting their stories right. Still, she couldn't help but feel nervous about actually acting out the engagement. It was so important they didn't let on that it was a charade. Nothing could be allowed to jeopardise the inheritance. There was too much at stake for their marriage to be revealed as a fraud.

Connor executed a perfect landing on the Garrison Downs airstrip and taxied the plane into the hangar. Rose was there to meet them in a four-by-four covered in red dust to take them to the house.

Her oldest sister was wearing jeans, riding boots, a checked shirt and an Akubra hat. She looked very much part of Garrison Downs in a hands-on, managerial manner. Apa had always told Ana how well Rose ran the show. Now Ana realised how fortunate she and her other sisters were to have her. Managing such an enormous enterprise as the cattle station was a task beyond her imaginings.

Without a moment's hesitation, Rose hugged Ana in greeting. No matter what Connor had warned, Ana truly believed in her sister's embrace of her into the family.

Ana introduced Rose to Connor. 'He and I have been friends since we were in primary school. I really wanted to show him Garrison Downs.'

'So pleased to meet you, Connor,' Rose said, with a firm handshake and a speculative glance.

When would be the right moment to tell Rose she and Connor were engaged? Ana had wanted to do it face to face, but somehow actually being with Rose made it seem more difficult. Announcing an engagement would usually happen in an organic way, because there would most likely be an existing relationship. Not by blurting out a hastily contrived plan.

The midday December sun blazed relentlessly down on them. Ana pulled her hat from her shoulder bag and jammed it on her head. It was a stylish city Panama, not a bushman's hat like Rose's. Like the other times she'd been to Garrison Downs, she felt out of place, intimidated by the vastness that surrounded her. She wore jeans, sturdy sneakers—not white; she'd had to throw her red-dust-stained white shoes out after her first visit—and a long-sleeved vintage shirt patterned with quirky representations of cacti. She couldn't pretend to be a rancher like Rose and Matilda, who had spent most of their lives here.

The night she and Connor had become 'engaged', Connor had asked her to read his mind. Now she got the feeling he was reading hers, because he took her hand and squeezed it reassuringly. It was if he sensed her feelings of inadequacy, a return to the private girls' high-school days, when she had felt intimidated by girls like her sisters, who were so sure of their place in the world. Not that Rose, Tilly or Eve had treated her with anything other than kindness and welcome.

She and Connor did not do holding hands. Now it seemed they did. For so many years she'd felt utterly at ease with him. Now she was confused. Was Connor holding her hand as an affectionate gesture because of their long-standing friendship, or as a ruse to appear authentic in their fake relationship? Whatever the reason, she liked the feeling. Although she knew she shouldn't get used to it. It would be too heart-breaking when Connor became her ex-husband and there would be no need for such false expressions of affection.

Rose focused on their clasped hands. She looked from Ana to Connor and back again. 'Ana, I forgot to ask. We've got the yellow suite ready for you. I know you were comfortable there the last two times you've visited.' She looked at Ana straight, with the same blue eyes Ana saw every time she looked in the mirror. 'Do you and Connor need two bedrooms or one?'

Ana hesitated, paralysed by indecision. She wanted to say, 'Two bedrooms, please'. The thought of sharing a bedroom with Connor suddenly became impossible. She could maybe stutter an explanation to Rose that they were waiting until their wedding night to share a bedroom, but Rose didn't know yet that they were getting married. And who would believe they'd wait? She closed her eyes firmly at a sudden, disconcerting image of Connor and her in bed, naked, sheets tangled around them.

No!

'One bedroom, please, Rose,' said Connor firmly. He still had hold of Ana's hand.

Rose looked again at the 'not just friends' way they were holding hands, then at Ana again. 'Ana, that ring—it's like a beacon. Does it mean—?'

'We're engaged,' Connor said with a big, Connor grin. 'You're the very first to know.'

'That's wonderful! Congratulations,' Rose said.

'Because me getting married is so important to Garrison Downs, we wanted to share the news with my sisters before we even told our families,' said Ana.

Ana could see her sister was genuinely pleased for her and Connor. But she sensed relief there too. Three sisters partnered now and only one to go, Rose herself. It was easy to imagine the pressure she must be feeling. Ana wanted to commiserate but, knowing how the husband hunt had worn her down, she didn't dare.

'I didn't know you were dating someone,' Rose said.

'I wasn't. I mean, we didn't date. Not in that sense, anyway. Connor isn't *someone*. He's my best friend. We hadn't seen each other for six months. And, when we did, we…er…realised our friendship had grown into something much deeper than…than friendship.'

Too much information, Ana.

'We realised we'd fallen in love,' said Connor, as if that was the simplest possible explanation. Which, of course, it was. Why hadn't she thought to say that, instead of rambling on?

Truth was, it cut too close. Ana had probably been more than a little in love with Connor for most of her life, but she could never admit it to herself. Hearing him say it was like a painful stab to her heart. Because he'd always made it so clear that he could never be in love with her. But she reassured herself that Connor's words weren't a total lie. It took a kind of love for her friend to go along with a fake marriage for her sake. Connor would get nothing at all from the arrangement. He was going along with the charade simply to help her out.

'Isn't this just the best news?' said Rose, smiling. 'Show me the ring.'

Ana splayed out her left hand. The diamonds glinted in the sunlight and looked very impressive. Quite the ring one would expect from a multi-millionaire fiancé.

'It's stunning. Did you make it?'

Ana shook her head. She had made both Tilly's and Eve's wedding rings. 'This is too complex for me—at the moment, anyway.'

'Eve and Tilly will be thrilled with your news. When are you planning to get married?'

There was a note of concern in Rose's voice that Ana, also driven to desperation by the need to find a man to marry, recognised. There were less than six months for them all to be wed.

'Well before the deadline set by the will,' she said. Then realised that, while that sounded reassuring, it didn't sound very romantic.

Connor jumped in. 'I've waited so long for her to grow up, we don't want to wait any longer to get married.'

Waited for her to grow up? What? She glared at him. She was only two years younger than he was. He could never resist teasing her. Still, his explanation sounded genuine, and that was all that counted.

'We thought a January wedding,' Ana said. 'Just a small one. Family and close friends.'

Australian law required at least a month's notice for a marriage. She had lodged the application the day after Connor had agreed to marry her. She wanted to be absolutely sure she was legally wed well before the deadline of the last day of May. After all, the will didn't state she had to spend time being engaged. It specified she had to be married. She wanted to get it done and dusted in plenty of time.

'Sounds great,' said Rose. 'Now, hop in the car and come on down to the house. Lunch is waiting for you. Clever of you to come by private plane, but it's still a long trip, and you must be hungry.'

Ana looked up at Connor. Their eyes met and they both burst into laughter. Rose looked somewhat taken aback. Ana hastened to reassure her. 'One thing you need to know about Connor is that he's always hungry.'

Rose laughed too. 'He won't go hungry here.'

This was Ana's third visit to Garrison Downs. She'd first come in June, for the read-

ing of the will, and to say farewell to her father
with a few private words at his graveside in the
family cemetery. Then just last month for Eve's
wedding to the super-hot Nate Harrington. She
had been thrilled to be her bridesmaid, along
with Rose and Tilly. The reason for the hasty
November wedding had immediately become
apparent: Eve was expecting a baby next June.
Ana, from having known no family on her father's side, could now look forward to being an
aunt, and she was delighted about it.

The newlyweds were waiting for Ana and
Connor at what the family called either the new
house or the homestead. Rose had already re-
layed the news about the engagement by phone,
so they were greeted with excited congratulations. Eve hugged Ana, and Connor too, when
Ana introduced him. The men shook hands.

Nate was the son of Holt's lawyer George
Harrington—keeper of all Apa's dealings regarding his secret daughter in Melbourne. Nate
had taken over his father's practice so, not only
was he now Ana's brother-in-law, but also the
Waverly family lawyer.

Eve was glowing. She was barely showing,
with just the tiniest of bumps, but it wasn't just
her blossoming pregnancy that seemed to have
softened the brittleness Ana had sensed in her

video call during the reading of the will. It was happiness too, and contentment.

When Eve had visited Ana in Melbourne, she had told her how, as a teenager, she had accidentally found out about Holt's past affair with Lili. Disillusioned and angry, she'd pretty much checked out of the Waverly family and gone to live with her mother's family in London as soon as she could. Now she was back, living at Garrison Downs for good. She and Nate were renovating the old house so they could live there—a move made after consultation with Ana.

The new house, opulent and elegant, made Ana feel again like she was stepping into the pages of a glossy design magazine. Page after page of large, high-ceilinged rooms with elaborate cornicing, cream walls and polished wooden floors. Everywhere she looked, she saw vignettes of immaculately styled antique and contemporary furniture, art and accessories. On her first visit, she'd thought it was the kind of French-inspired mansion she'd expect to see in Toorak, the wealthiest part of Melbourne, not in the middle of the South Australian desert. Yet, in a gesture towards the Australian climate, it was surrounded by wide verandas and shade-giving trees.

According to her sisters, the house was pure Rosamund. Her daughters hadn't changed the

interior design since their mother had died seven
years ago. Why would they? The house was a
masterpiece. But it was here, in this house that
had been Rosamund's haven, where Ana most
felt like an interloper. She doubted that her name
on the deed would change that.

Eve and Rose led her and Connor into the
family dining room. Thankfully, she was seated
with her back to the large portrait by a famous
artist of her father, his wife and three daughters that dominated the wall. It had been painted
when the girls had been pre-teens, showing a
joyous, united family.

Holt's real family.

It was a beautiful piece of art, and she knew
she shouldn't let it bother her. But she couldn't
help but let the portrait feed her feelings of ex-
clusion and lack of belonging.

Rose noticed. 'I'm sorry, Ana. I'd meant to
have that picture moved before your visit. We
can't very well paint you into it at this stage.
It's now no longer relevant.'

'But that was your family as it was then. A
slice of history. You don't need to move it for
my sake.'

'We do,' Eve said firmly. 'This is your home
too now, just as much as it is ours. I suggested
we commission a new painting of all four Waverly sisters to replace it.'

'We've talked about that with Tilly,' explained Rose. 'We all think it's a good idea. A new painting for new beginnings.'

Ana felt moved at her sisters' thoughtfulness. 'I'd like that. But you don't need to move this one,' she protested. 'Really. I do have my own lovely family in Melbourne.'

But not her father.

She paused. 'And I had Connor too.'

Always, she'd had Connor. And she couldn't let this fake engagement mess up their long friendship. Because she couldn't imagine life without Connor.

'Nah, it's toast,' said Rose in her no-nonsense way, although she accompanied her words with a wink. She got up to go to the kitchen to confer with the housekeeper about lunch.

Eve turned to Connor. 'I heard all about you, Connor, when I had dinner with Ana's family at the restaurant,' she said. 'But I believed you were the best of platonic friends. Now you're engaged?' She looked to Ana, her eyebrows raised.

Eve was astute. But Ana had a story and she was sticking to it. She looked up at Connor. It wasn't difficult to make it a loving glance as he really *was* her dearest friend. She was glad and grateful to have him here supporting her.

She took a deep breath. 'As I told Rose, Connor had been working in Sydney for six months. When we saw each other again, well, it was somehow different. We…we fell in love.' And she had to be constantly on her guard that she didn't really develop deeper feelings for him.

Just friends.

'We'd been friends for twenty years,' said Connor. 'But friendship was no longer enough. I asked her to marry me. Fortunately, she said yes.'

Connor smiled, then dipped his head to kiss Ana lightly on the mouth. It was the perfect thing for a fiancé to do. Possessive. Protective. Confident she would welcome his kiss. He hadn't kissed her since that first time when she'd been sixteen. She closed her eyes at the sheer bliss of it.

Connor was kissing her and she was loving it.

She returned the pressure of his mouth, aching for more. Then realised where she was and pulled back. She forced an easy smile to hide her bewilderment at the strong feelings that simple kiss had evoked. She must not let herself want more than friendship from him.

'Oh, my!' To Ana's surprise, Eve gave a breathy exclamation and blinked back tears. She snatched up a napkin and dabbed at her eyes. 'Ignore me, my hormones are all over the place. That kiss… You two really do look perfect together. To think, two of us are married and you are engaged, and all with six months to go…'

Eve's gaze drifted to Rose's vacated seat. 'Although I don't want to put any pressure on Rose. We've all been lucky to do it for love. The idea that she would have to…' She dabbed at her eyes again. Nate put his arm around his wife and smiled at Ana.

Ana scarcely heard Eve, too lost in a mist of sensual euphoria from Connor's kiss. Connor cleared his throat. Was he as affected by that brief touch of his lips on hers as she was? Or was he embarrassed? It was all very well in theory to talk about feigning physical affection to make their relationship appear believable. The actual practice wasn't so straightforward.

She would be sharing a bedroom with Connor.

How was she going to manage that and the intimacy it implied?

CHAPTER SIX

CONNOR LOOKED AROUND him as he strode away from the homestead. As far as he could see, and far beyond, lay the land belonging to Garrison Downs—one and a half million hectares of it. The landholding of a billionaire cattle baron. Land that encompassed lush grazing, bushland and scrubland. He imagined the wildflowers would be spectacular in spring, transforming the landscape into a riot of colour. He'd been told a river that ran through rocky outcrops, as well as underground bores, brought water to even the furthest paddocks. He took a deep breath, filling his lungs with the clean air scented with eucalypt, and another more earthy, familiar smell that let him know that stables were nearby.

Nothing Ana had told him about the place had prepared him for how it felt to actually be at Garrison Downs and take in the magnificence of the property. For Ana to be a part owner would be a privilege beyond measure. He felt suffused with the energy and determination to help her find her rightful place here. It wasn't just immense wealth the sisters would gain but also responsibility as caretakers of this land.

Ana still felt intimidated by her inheritance and all that came with it. That was understandable, considering the circumstances. He wanted to help her embrace what Garrison Downs could mean to her. Family. Connection. Freedom. And a place to ground her when life got tough in the city. All this was hers to share with her sister. With enough funds for it to run smoothly and to keep on delivering a torrent of dollars to her bank account. It made him happy that Ana had finally been acknowledged by her father. But how much longer would she have had to wait if he had not died prematurely?

Connor had met Holt Waverly on a few occasions, as the best friend next door who was in on the secret of Ana's birth. Her elusive father had been a towering, robust man. Handsome in a rugged way. A deep, booming voice that resonated authority. A man of the land who strode the city streets with confidence. Sure of himself to the point of arrogance. Connor had liked the man, although he was not sure he admired him. He had not liked how sad his daughter always was after her father went off home to his world of Garrison Downs. A world that Ana could never share. Until now. Thankfully her father had left his secret daughter a legacy of recognition, part-ownership of this magnificent place, and—arguably most important—sisters.

Eve and Rose appeared to be everything Ana believed them to be. Connor liked them a lot— Nate too. He hadn't expected that. He had counselled Ana to be wary. To watch out for ways the sisters might try to minimise her share of the inheritance. To expect they might ditch her after the inheritance was disbursed. Now Connor was willing to admit he could have been wrong. The sisterly love seemed genuine. He could see Ana's confidence flourishing. Not just because of the hand of sisterhood the three women had extended but also because, through his will, her father had formally acknowledged her importance to him and her right to be a Waverly and be part of Garrison Downs.

Connor would do what he did best—look out for Ana. It was what he had always done. And what he would continue to do for as long as she needed him.

As a friend.

He had agreed to the marriage of convenience scheme to help her. Privately, he'd had his lawyers look at the will, only for them to agree with the lawyers the sisters had engaged.

There was no way out of that archaic clause requiring marriage for the four sisters.

But there was danger in the benign agreement between he and Ana that he hadn't anticipated. Kissing Ana had been like lighting a fuse which had set off a series of explosions that had rocked him. Lust. Desire. An urge to possess her.

He wanted her.

He'd wanted her for a long time. But above that, on an entirely different plane, he cared for her. He had seen the wonderful person she was even as a child. That admiration for her, that looking out for her, that *friendship* had endured. He didn't want to lose their friendship, which wasn't tainted by the unrealistic expectations and disappointments of a romantic relationship. He never wanted to hurt her the way he knew he had hurt the girlfriends he could not commit to.

Although he always tried to be honest with them. There was something about a man who said he didn't want commitment that was like a flag to a certain kind of woman—like Brandi.

He and his business partners in The Money Club thought of themselves as low-key nerds who had never courted publicity. Somehow, Brandi had heard of them and tracked him down. What had seemed to be a spontaneous meeting in a bar in Melbourne had actually been a calculated hunt. Ana had sensed something not right about Brandi from the get-go. He should have listened to her. She knew him better than anyone. He'd thought she might be jealous. Instead it had turned out she'd been right.

He knew Ana was attracted to him. She had been aware of him as a man long before he'd been aware of her as a woman. He could not take advantage of her vulnerability. Ana was not the woman for a fling. Especially not a fling with him, a man who cared about her. A man who wanted to keep her in his life. A man who didn't want to risk losing her for the sake of a sexual interlude because they were forced into proximity in a fake relationship. He did not want Ana to be another woman's phone number deleted from his phone and his life.

'Connor, wait up. We're nearly there,' Ana called.

Lost in his thoughts, he hadn't realised he'd got so far ahead of Ana and Rose on their way to the stables, which were some distance from the house. They were keeping pace with the beautiful old border collie, River, who was accompanying them. River was very old, with a stiff-legged gait that spoke of arthritis. When Connor had petted him, he'd given him a surreptitious examination for any of the suspicious lumps and bumps that could be found on a dog this age. All clear. His eyes were good for a dog so old, and his teeth too. Connor was relieved. Ana had already become very fond of Holt's canine friend. River was a remaining link with her father. There should be some good years still left in the old boy.

'Ana tells me she's picked out horses for us both,' he said to Rose.

Ana had told him how their mutual love of horses had helped her bond with Tilly, Eve and Rose. That they'd realised they had more in common than their blue eyes.

'She did indeed,' said Rose. 'You'll be riding Zircon and we've put Ana on Ruby. Can you ride with a stock saddle?'

'Yep. So can Ana. We learned to ride Western as well as English.'

'She told me you learned together when you were kids.'

'Kept us out of trouble,' he said. Their shared love of horses had also helped keep their friendship flourishing.

'Did Ana tell you that we went on a junior jackaroo and jillaroo school holiday camp when she was fourteen and I was sixteen? We were both very keen to go and pestered our parents until they agreed.'

'My mother worked in an office full-time and

Connor's parents were busy doctors,' Ana said to Rose. 'They were always looking for holiday care for us. We didn't have to pester them too hard to get us off their hands.'

'My whole life here was like a jackaroo camp,' Rose said with a laugh. 'I reckon I was in training to be a stockman from the time I could walk.'

'And you loved it, didn't you, Rose?' Ana said.

'I resented every minute I was away from here,' Rose said. 'Garrison Downs is my life, and I will do anything to keep it in our hands.'

The three of them fell silent. Connor could tell Ana was aching to tell Rose about their marriage-of-convenience idea. But they'd agreed that they couldn't take any risk of their marriage being declared fraudulent. It was best to keep quiet about it.

'Although Ana might appear the perfect city slicker, she is very at home on horseback,' he said. 'Years of pony club on the outskirts of Melbourne and holiday horse camps.'

'Nothing was as good as the jillaroo camp,' Ana said. 'It was held at a working cattle station in the west of Victoria. Nothing on this scale, of course. We slept in bunk beds in an old barn. I thought I'd gone to heaven.'

'Me too,' Connor said. 'We didn't just ride and

look after horses, we also learned how to muster sheep and cattle.'

'So I can put you to work here, Connor?' Rose said with a grin.

'My skills are a little rusty,' he said with an answering grin.

'I bet you haven't forgotten how to lasso a steer or crack a stock whip,' said Ana.

'You were pretty good at cracking a stock whip, if I recall,' he said. She was so petite but she'd been determined to make that whip crack, and she had.

'My grandmother went hysterical when she heard I'd been cracking whips,' said Ana. 'She thought it was dangerous and told my mother off for letting me go to the camp.'

'She didn't know the half of it,' Connor said. 'We were fearless. We wanted to try everything. We didn't care if it was dangerous.'

'We were always supervised,' Ana said primly.

He laughed. 'Yeah. Right. Remember when you and that other girl decided you wanted to ride a pig and sneaked off on your own? Luckily it was a sweet, tame pig or it could have ended differently.'

'You tried to ride a pig?' said Rose. 'Bareback?'

'Of course bareback. They didn't have pig saddles.'

'She slid off into the mud,' said Connor. 'I remember it so well.'

'He doesn't let me forget it,' Ana said.

'And I never will,' he said.

'The owners weren't happy and threatened to send us home,' Ana said. 'They made us clean out the chicken shed, which wasn't as much fun as riding a pig.'

'But just as smelly,' said Connor.

Ana flushed and laughed. She looked as cute as she had covered in mud when she'd been thirteen. Those were times when he'd still thought of Ana as a sister. He hadn't thought that way after that first kiss at her school formal. But he'd refused to acknowledge the change in his feelings. Platonic friendship was the way to keep her in his life.

'Sounds like fun,' said Rose.

'I'm grateful for those experiences because, although it was kid stuff, it means I'm not completely ignorant about how a farm works,' Ana said. 'Although nothing could prepare me for the scale of Garrison Downs.'

She turned to Connor. 'Remember how excited you were when you were allowed to give a vaccine injection to a horse? Under supervision, of course.' She turned back to Rose. 'I think Connor first got the idea he wanted to be a vet then, although he's never said that. At that stage he was still set on becoming a doctor, the family profession.'

'Did you go back to the jackaroo camp?' asked Rose.

'The next year my grandparents took me to visit Budapest.' Ana pronounced it 'Buda*pesht*'. 'My grandmother wanted me to have other influences. She didn't think whip-cracking was a safe or ladylike thing to do. Good thing I never told her about the pig.'

'Budapest? Is that where your grandparents were from? What was visiting there like?'

'Awesome. Budapest is the most beautiful city you can imagine. So sophisticated to my fifteen-year-old eyes. It was like stepping into a different world for me. I loved it.'

'Did you have family there?'

'Yes. My great-uncle owns a jewellery store. It was a revelation. That's where I really got interested in jewellery. His daughter has a gorgeous fashion boutique near the opera house. She took me in hand and helped me to choose clothes that suited me and how to wear them. I had such fun.'

'Ana came back quite the girly girl,' Connor said.

He remembered how shocked he'd been. She'd had her hair styled differently, and for a moment he hadn't recognised her, only to acknowledge how lovely she was. His buddy had grown up.

As they got closer to the stables, Ana tried to recall the last time she'd gone horse-riding with Connor. It was well before he'd headed off to Sydney. It wasn't that their interest in horses had waned, more that different, more accesible activities had intruded as they'd grown up. Particularly at weekends.

She'd moved high school for the final two years, away from the bitchiness of the girls' school, with its popular girl cult which had totally excluded her, to another private school. Apa had insisted she attend private schools and, as he'd paid the school fees, her mother hadn't argued. The new, co-educational school had been closer to home, more laid back and inclusive. She'd been so much happier, although she'd continued the fiction that her father was dead. She'd made other friends and got involved with school sport, playing competitive tennis at the weekend to cement new friendships.

There'd been an increase in study load, particularly for Connor, striving to get into medicine. The university course required an incredibly high mark for entry. When her time had come for final year studies, she'd buckled down too.

Horse riding had become a special treat rather than a regular routine.

Now she was excited at the prospect of riding with him again, and on Waverly land. She and Connor had changed into their riding boots back at the house. They carried their helmets with them. It looked much cooler to be on horseback wearing just an Akubra hat. But neither of them rode without a protective helmet, especially on an unfamiliar horse. Connor's parents had insisted. They'd seen too many head injuries to allow otherwise.

The Garrison Downs stables was a substantial complex. As well as the working horses for the stockmen, there were the family horses, and the valuable stud horses. As they neared the stable, Sally, the stable manager, rushed out to greet them.

'Rose, glad you're here!' Sally said. 'I'm worried about Jasper. He's gone lame—front right hoof. He's obviously in pain.'

Connor looked at Ana. She nodded. 'You know Connor is a vet?' she said to Rose.

'I'd be happy to look at Jasper,' Connor said.

Jasper had been Holt's horse and Ana knew he was particularly precious to Rose. 'I couldn't bear it if anything happened to him, Ana,' she said. Rose untied and tied her ponytail, something Ana noticed she did when she was troubled.

Ana put a hand on Rose's arm. 'I know. But Jasper is in good hands with Connor.'

Jasper was a black stallion of more than seventeen hands. He was very obviously lame. 'He's the sweetest boy,' said Rose, stroking the horse's face. 'He'll behave for you. He likes men. Dad raised him from a foal.'

Connor rolled up his shirtsleeves to reveal his strong, tanned forearms. He washed his hands then donned surgical gloves from the large, well-stocked equine first-aid cupboard. Jasper nickered a greeting when Connor approached him. Ana watched as Connor spoke to the big horse in a low, soothing voice. 'Let me have a look at that hoof that's causing you so much trouble.'

Jasper let Connor examine his hoof. 'I'm looking for evidence of a puncture, a stone bruise, laminitis, cracks, white line disease.' After a long moment, he looked up to Rose. 'I've found the problem. An abscess, which is a build-up of pus and infection within the hoof.'

'I've treated abscesses before,' said Sally, the stable manager. 'I know what to do.'

'Sally is a trained veterinary nurse,' Rose said.

'Good,' said Connor. 'Do you know how to get his shoe off?'

'I can do that,' said Sally.

'Then we need to get his hoof into a bucket of warm water with Epsom salts and iodine. The solution will encourage the abscess to burst so it can drain.'

'I can do better than a bucket,' said Sally. 'Holt bought a special boot for the horses that we can pull up over his hoof and fill with the solution.'

'Excellent,' said Connor. 'Then we apply a poultice, using a drawing cream to help or—'

'We have drawing treatment, bandages and tape for the poultice,' said Rose. 'We've got antibiotics too, anti-inflammatories and pain medication if you think Jasper might need them. We're a long way from the nearest vet, and have to be prepared for emergencies.'

Ana watched with growing respect as Connor worked. He was so competent. So reassuring. And kind. He knew how upset Rose and Sally were at seeing this beloved animal in pain. He reassured them, as well as murmuring a litany of soothing words to the horse. Her heart swelled with affection for him. She was proud of him. There was a new assurance to her friend, an air of authority that he knew exactly what he was doing and that he was doing it well. He was…extraordinary in every way. It made him even more desirable. If she allowed herself to think of him in that way.

Once the poultice was on, Connor turned to Rose. 'I'll check on Jasper again this evening. Then again in the morning and before we leave after lunch. After that, it will be your call if you need to contact your vet.'

Rose hugged him. 'You're going to be an asset to Garrison Downs, Connor. I don't suppose you'd consider moving here after you're married, as our resident vet?' She was joking, Ana knew, but there was a note of seriousness there too. Connor certainly looked the country boy in his moleskin trousers and checked shirt. But then he looked perfect in the city too. Darn it, Connor looked the part wherever he was. She dreaded the moment she would have to tell her sisters she and Connor were getting divorced.

'That would be entirely up to Ana,' he said. 'Garrison Downs would be an awesome place to live.'

Ana clenched her hand around the strap of her helmet. Was he serious? Or was he playing along with the premise that they would be married in a month and that him living here could be a possibility? The further they got into this charade, the more difficult it would be for both of them not to blur the boundaries.

Did she want to live at Garrison Downs? It was too early to tell. Besides, she wasn't yet married, and neither was Rose. There was no guarantee owning Garrison Downs would actually happen. What was that old saying? 'Don't count your chickens until they're hatched.'

One of the stable hands had Ruby, a sweet-natured chestnut mare, saddled ready for Ana to ride. A handsome bay gelding, Zircon, was ready for Connor. The stable hand had warmed the horses up for them on the sand arena.

Once Ana and Connor were mounted, Rose gave them directions for a ride to the river. She gave Ruby a friendly pat on the rump and told Ana she'd see them back at the homestead when they were ready.

The ride took them past the well-tended private graveyard known as Prospect Hill where her father was buried under the shade of a flame tree. Both she and Connor dismounted to pay their respects. The last time she'd been here with Rose, she'd been too overwhelmed with grief over her loss to notice anything about the other graves. This time she saw that Rosamund was also buried there. Holt's parents were too, Katherine and Cecil Waverly.

'Your middle name is Katherine,' Connor said as he examined the headstone with her.

'Apa insisted I have a middle name from his family. I always liked having that connection. Now I'm told by my sisters Katherine could be cantankerous and domineering and gave their mother, her daughter-in-law, hell.' She laughed.

Connor laughed too. 'You're not cantankerous and domineering, so that's all that counts. Well, I guess you can be cantankerous when you want to be.'

'Careful, or I'll show you cantankerous,' she said, punching him lightly on his arm, laughter still lingering. 'It's interesting, though, to find out about this side of my family. I've never known anything about them. If you remember, Garrison Downs was won in a poker game by my great-great-grandmother. Imagine that. She must have been one feisty woman. Tilly is a historian—she's Dr Waverly, you know. Her speciality is old letters. Wouldn't it be great if she could find out more about the Waverly ancestors?'

'What would be really great is if she found evidence enough to ditch that punitive clause in the will.'

Ana laughed. 'Trust you to describe marriage as *punitive*.'

He smiled. 'Point taken. But I don't deny it. You know my views on marriage. Don't tell me that requirement hasn't caused you a lot of stress.'

'Thanks to you, some of that stress has been lifted. Now I worry for Rose.'

'You've become attached to your sisters, haven't you?'

She nodded. 'Very much so. But I'm still not sure that I belong. I'm trying to adjust to the massive change Apa's will has brought to my life. My sisters have such a deep sense of birth right and attachment to this place. I'm not sure they could ever understand where I come from. What it was like to have our father drop in and out of my life. How I coped by telling people my father was dead. How I was his dirty little secret.'

'Don't call yourself that,' Connor said, frowning.

'It's true, though.' She looked towards Rosamund's headstone. 'Their mother had to be protected at all costs from knowing about me, as if I was something to be ashamed of. She would never have let me set foot on the property.'

'From what you know from your mother, Rosamund had pushed Holt away. Didn't want him near her. They were on the brink of divorce. That's why he fell for Lili.'

'Not quite as simple as that, according to my sisters. It's only since Apa died that Tilly discovered her mother's diaries.'

'Hidden diaries? The plot thickens.'

Ana nodded. 'So much fell into place for them. They had never been told about Lili and certainly not about me. Eve found out about Lili accidentally when she was fifteen, but she didn't tell anyone. She hated the hypocrisy of them presenting as the perfect marriage, when in fact the marriage had been far from perfect. When she finished school, she went to live in London and it caused a family rift.

'The diaries showed that Rosamund suffered undiagnosed severe post-natal depression after Tilly's birth. Both she and Holt were deeply unhappy, their marriage on the rocks. That's when Holt found comfort and love with Mum. But, when Rosamund was finally diagnosed and treated, Holt ended his affair with my mother and gave their marriage a second chance. Apparently they were then very happy.'

Connor went quiet and Ana realised this talk of infidelity must be hitting a raw nerve for him. 'I'm sorry. I hope hearing about people being unfaithful doesn't bring back memories.'

'Yeah. It does. It reinforces my reasons for not wanting to get married—lack of trust being the biggie. How could Holt's wife ever trust him again? How could your mother trust another man?'

'We don't know about Rosamund. But, although my mum didn't date much at all until after I left school, she did meet Ben, and they're very happy.'

'This case is different from my parents' story,' Connor said. 'Holt and his wife worked together to repair their marriage. My father was a serial cheater, going right back to the early days of their marriage. There were multiple liaisons.'

'And you were the one to—'

'Catch him out with one of his support staff. And I didn't have the guts to tell my mother.' He kicked against a stray weed with his riding boot. That was at the core of the damage inflicted on him by his parents' divorce. And Ana was the only person with whom he'd shared the trauma that he'd known what his father was up to. But he hadn't been able to bring himself to tell his mother.

'You were sixteen years old. It wasn't your place. Besides, you did tell her, in a way, by warning your father if he didn't come clean with your mother you would let her know what you'd discovered. It was brave of you.'

'After it all exploded, I was left with the suspicion that Mum had known all along about the other women but didn't want to confront it. I don't think she's ever forgiven me for disturbing the status quo.'

'Again, not your fault.'

'Maybe it was. Maybe it wasn't. But I'm like him, Ana. You know that. I look like him. People mistake our voices on the phone. What if I am as incapable of fidelity as he is? Unable to be trusted? If I ever married and had kids, I wouldn't want them to go through what Billy and I did.'

His face was contorted with anguish. It tore at Ana's heart. Even now, he tormented himself over what he saw as his role in the break-up of his family. And that history might repeat itself if he married. If only he could see how wrong he was. He did look like his father but that was as far as it went. His father was superficially charming. She'd liked him and he'd been kind to her as a child. But Connor was the real deal, genuine in a way his father wasn't. The father was the one with the problem, not the son.

Why had his mother let Connor blame himself the way he had? So many times Ana had tried to comfort him and reason with him that he was tormenting himself for no purpose.

'As I've said before, you are not your father. Not anything like him in everything but looks. Listen to me, who has known you for most of your life—I've never had any cause to distrust you.' She paused. 'Have you ever cheated on your girlfriends?'

'Never,' he said. 'But I can't give them what they want.'

'Because it's not what you want. You haven't met the right person yet. When you do—'

'People start off marriage thinking they've met the right person. Where's the guarantee in that?' he said.

'There can't be guarantees. My grandmother says you can never see inside someone else's marriage to know what's really happening.'

'Your grandparents are an example of a good marriage,' Connor said.

'Yes, they are. They fell in love when they were eighteen. They went through hardships we can't even imagine, but their love kept them going And I know lots of people in what appear to be happy marriages.'

'And just as many that suddenly explode when the cheating is revealed.'

His mouth had a cynical twist she didn't like to see on his handsome face. She needed to kill this conversation. 'What would I know?' she said. 'I'm twenty-five and don't have the slightest interest in getting married. Not yet. You're twenty-seven and haven't found the right person yet. Fortunately for me, you're free to help me out in this weird situation, where I have to get married whether I like it or not.'

'What are friends for?' he said flatly.

'Indeed.' She choked out the word through a suddenly constricted throat.

Friends. He could never see her as anything more than a platonic pal.

He was silent for a long moment. She knew him so well, she could see he was forcing himself out of his dark moment. Connor being Connor, he had to hug all that pain to himself.

'Seeing all this makes me very glad I'm helping you—in my own hire-a-hubby way—and your sisters to claim what is rightfully yours.' He waved his arm to encompass their surroundings. 'Garrison Downs is worth it. It's a prize beyond value.'

'And I'm very grateful.'

The more Ana thought about what she'd asked of Connor, the more she realised what a big deal it was. She had pretty well asked him to put his private life on hold for more than a year. Though, once they were married, he could discreetly date…

No! She clenched her fists by her sides. She couldn't bear the thought of him being with another woman. Nausea rose in her throat. She had to fight that thought with all she had.

For how long had she been kidding herself? *She wanted him—and not just as a friend.* But it couldn't happen. Not when all the feelings were only on her side.

Rose had showed her where a cleared track of red dirt wound up a rise to the lookout over the river. 'Right now, I want to take advantage of us having these beautiful horses to ride. What do you say?'

'I say race you up that track to the lookout.'

They quickly mounted their horses again.

'Starting from now,' Connor said.

Rose laughed. 'Game on! C'mon, Ruby.'

Rose had always wanted her own horse. She'd found her in Ruby. The mare was beautifully trained, responsive, strong and good-natured. Ruby was a dream come true. Another reason to make sure her marriage of convenience helped to ensure the inheritance.

She reached the lookout just behind Connor. He looked so good on horseback, relaxed, in control, as one with his mount. There was something very appealing—okay, say it—something *sexy*, about a handsome, well-built man who could control a strong, powerful animal with skill and kindness. He would never use spurs or a whip. Neither would she, of course. She wondered if somehow her lack of success with men was because they could never live up to Connor.

They slowed their horses to a walk when the incline became steeper. The view that opened up to them from their vantage point on a rocky outcrop of red sandstone made her catch her breath. The shadows of the opposing stony ridges were starting to lengthen. Down below them, the

slow-moving river, its waters blue in the afternoon sun, snaked through banks of large peb-
bles, eucalypts and scrub. A ghost gum, which
had most likely been hit and killed by light-
ning, stood proud, its bare white branches stark
against the greenery. A flock of pink Major
Mitchell cockatoos took flight, swooping by,
the sun glinting on their wings, their raucous
cries breaking the silence of the landscape.

'Wow!' Ana breathed. 'What else can I say?'

'Anything you and your sisters have to do
to retain ownership of this place will be worth
it,' Connor said, sounding almost reverential.

She turned Ruby to face him. 'You've fallen
for Garrison Downs, haven't you?'

'Who wouldn't?' he said.

Maybe me, she thought. The property was
truly magnificent. The income would bring her
wealth beyond her wildest dreams. But would
she want to actually live here, like Rose and
Eve? It was so isolated for a person whose home
ground was Melbourne.

'I see a trail going down to the water,' she
said. 'Shall we take the horses down? I reckon
some of that water is shallow enough to ride
them through. They'll love splashing through it.'

'So will we. Can you imagine how much
we would have loved this place when we were

kids? You wouldn't have been able to keep us away.'

Kids. Children at Garrison Downs. Eve was expecting a baby next June. Tilly would soon, no doubt, be expected to bear an heir to the throne of Chaleur. And her? Kids weren't anywhere on her radar. Not now. So why when she imagined her future children here, happy on horseback, did she see a little green-eyed boy who looked just like Connor?

CHAPTER SEVEN

ANA HAD NEVER felt more awkward with Connor than she did standing with him in the air-conditioned splendour of the yellow suite. *Their* room.

They'd just got back from their ride on Ruby and Zircon, which had ended in an exhilarating gallop back to the stables. Connor had checked on Jasper before they'd headed back to the house. Such luxury to leave the horses with the stable hands to take off their saddles and bridles, wash them down and groom them. Although, on the walk back to the house, she and Connor had agreed that they actually liked that time with their horses after a ride. Next visit, she'd allow enough time to look after Ruby herself.

She and Connor had pulled off their riding boots in the mudroom on the way in. Now she stood with him in the bedroom in their socked feet on the pale, floral patterned rug. It was the first time she'd shared a bedroom with him since she'd been, maybe, seven years old and bunked down with both O'Neill brothers when his parents had been babysitting her.

The suite comprised a large, elegant bedroom with a king-sized bed, a study area with a chaise longue style sofa, over-stuffed arm chairs and a full-sized en suite bathroom. Her gaze kept being drawn to that bed.

She couldn't share a bed with Connor.

No bed could be big enough. Not, she realised, to save herself from Connor. But to save Connor from her. She was on guard while she was awake. But she couldn't guarantee that she could continue to dam her feelings of attraction to him if they had to sleep together in the same bed. And that could lead to disaster for their fake marriage plans.

The suite had obviously been designed with excellent taste and a big budget. The crisp, high-thread-count linen was in tasteful shades of lemon and white with piles of coordinating cushions. Framed botanical prints of wildflowers adorned the walls. It was like a suite in a luxury hotel, with everything provided for a guest's comfort. Ana admired its beauty, though she preferred a less fussy style.

That bed!

It dominated the room. She had to force herself to look away from it. Was Connor feeling as edgy as she was?

Connor being Connor, he didn't show it. 'Man, this is such a girly room,' he said, looking around him. 'In fact, this entire house is not exactly guy-friendly.'

He had a point. 'Maybe,' she said. She didn't want to criticise anything about the interior of the house. Because that could be seen as criticising Rosamund, and she couldn't be drawn into anything like that.

'I can't imagine your father coming into the house and kicking off his boots after a day mustering cattle. Especially in that room with the white carpet.'

'I guess that's what the mudroom is for. To kick off the boots, I mean, like we did. But Apa's study is very much a guy room.'

'It's very much *his* room. How many portraits of the man can there be? It seems a bit—'

'Self-important?' She hardly dared voice the words. She had adored her father. But she hadn't known the public side of him. There were some high-powered people in those photos with Holt on the walls of his study. Her father had been so respected, he'd been given a state funeral.

'You said it,' Connor said.

'I really like his study,' she said. 'I feel close to him there. It's likely my sisters feel the same.

To be fair, I don't know if that overtly masculine décor was him or Rosamund. Or whether it was him or her who wanted to hang that multitude of portraits and photos. The house was her domain. From what I knew of Apa, he would have let her do what she wanted. The outdoors was his domain.'

'It was good of Rose to have that family portrait moved,' Connor said. 'That showed sensitivity and thoughtfulness. I like her.'

'I thought you would. I was touched by how considerate she is. And what a great idea to get a portrait painted of all four of us, though when we'll all be together I don't know. Tilly was only here a few weeks ago for Eve's wedding. It's not like she can drop her royal duties and fly all the way down here for a girls' lunch.'

'True,' he said.

'Rose seems to be very much the outdoors type, like Apa. I don't think she pays too much attention to the finer points of interior design.' She looked up at him. 'However, she might want to make changes to the house. Why don't you ask her about it over dinner?'

'No thanks. I'll avoid contentious topics. I'll be too busy making sure I say the right thing about our engagement. It would be only too easy to slip up.'

'Connor, you're doing great. You actually fit

in here better than I do. I thought Sally was going to swoon when she was watching you tend to Jasper. Seriously, you're a big hit with everyone.'

'That's only because they care about you. As it should be. They want you to be happy.'

'I guess. But I worry that after we—'

'After we get divorced it might be messy?'

'No. I—'

'I know you, Ana. That is precisely what you were thinking. What comes after doesn't matter. It's now that counts. Establishing our credentials as a genuine couple. Moving towards the wedding next month. Afterwards, I can be the villain.'

'You could never be cast as a villain, Connor. You will always be the hero. To…to me anyway.' She paused and looked up at him to meet his green eyes. His hair was all tousled from where he'd run his fingers through it after he'd taken off his helmet. He'd never looked more handsome. 'I wish…' She stopped herself. For a scary moment there, an uncalled-for thought had clamoured to be voiced.

I wish we were a couple for real.

He met her gaze intently. 'You wish—?' There was an edge to his question she didn't recognise.

Flustered, she stepped back. Her words

spilled out. 'I… I…wish we had two bathrooms here, because I'd like a shower.'

'That's it?' he said, frowning. 'That's your wish?'

She took a step back from him. 'Er. Yes. It was hot out there. I feel sticky and probably smell of horse.'

He laughed. 'If you do, I do too.' He paused. 'Do you want me to ask Rose can I use a different bathroom?'

'No. Please.' Ana put her hand on his arm. 'That would be giving the game away. Do you mind if I shower first? I'm sure I'll take longer to get ready for dinner than you will.'

'Go for it,' he said. 'And I won't say take as long as you want to, because I know you will anyway.'

'You'll never forgive me for using all the hot water at horse camp, will you?'

'That was so long ago. Do I hold grudges? There's nothing I love more than a freezing cold shower in an open barn in the middle of winter.'

Connor paced the room. What kind of torture was it to share a bedroom with Ana? Wherever he turned, that big bed was in sight. But the worst torture imaginable was hearing the shower going and knowing Ana was naked in there behind those glass doors.

He didn't have to work hard to imagine her soaping her body, twisting and turning under the water. He had to dial back on the fantasy of opening that bathroom door and offering to wash her back for her. Perhaps joining her under the water... He shook his head to clear it of such untoward thoughts.

He had never seen Ana naked. Why would he have? They were *friends*. Friends kept their clothes on. When they were children, he and Billy had cheerfully run around without a stitch on but Ana had always been modest.

He paced some more. She was taking for ever in there—he would have been in and out of the shower in five minutes—but that was what girly girls did. He wouldn't have her any other way.

He couldn't remember when he'd last enjoyed a day so much. He could be completely relaxed in Ana's company—even when she confronted him about his attitude to marriage. Even then, he knew she understood him and cared for him. That criticism came from a warm place in her heart. Fact was, he had never felt so at ease with any other woman. Perhaps because there was no romantic relationship between them, there were no unrealistic expectations on either side. No demands. No manoeuvring for change. Whatever her magic was, he felt happy when he was with Ana. It was a good feeling.

Ana had always been there for him. And he would drop everything to be there for her. Realistically, he knew that could not go on for ever. Not when possible future partners might come between them. It was irrational of him to want it to. But he found it difficult to imagine life without his long-time friend. Those weeks when he'd cut her off for criticising Brandi hadn't been fun. In fact, he'd been miserable. It wasn't until he'd walked into the restaurant that night to see Ana there that his spirits had finally lifted.

He heard the glass bathroom door open. He turned his back to it and stepped away, as a gentleman should when a lady who was not his lover emerged from the bathroom. There was a possibility she might be wearing only a towel that didn't do a good job of covering her. Or a skimpy little robe that fell open as she moved, revealing tantalising glimpses of slender thighs and high, firm breasts.

No glimpses for him.

Not even the tiniest peek.

This was Ana.

He focused resolutely on a painting of a pretty, purple wildflower. He had no clue as to what it was. He could identify indigenous animals but flowers weren't his thing. Ana liked them, though. He'd been away for her last birthday so had sent her flowers. She'd been inordinately thrilled with them.

Her voice came from behind him. Towel or robe? 'You seem very interested in that flower,' she said.

'Not really. I was just turning my back to give you a chance to get out of the bathroom. In case you, uh—'

'Didn't have any clothes on?'

'Uh...yes.' She was pretty good at reading his mind. But he wouldn't want her to be party to the fantasies he'd been having about her.

'I took my clothes in with me so I could get dressed there. I'm decent. You can turn around.'

She stood there, face flushed, eyes so blue they hardly seemed real, hair tumbling to her shoulders. She was wearing a short black dress with thin straps that skimmed her curves.

'You look lovely,' he said, suddenly short of breath.

'You know what they say, Melbourne girls only wear black. Can't disappoint people.'

'You would never disappoint anyone.'

'Th...thank you,' she said, looking up at him.

Their gazes held for a long time. He took a step closer without breaking eye contact. 'Would now be a good time to practise kissing?'

She stood very still. 'There's no one to witness it. So...what would be the point?'

'We don't want to look like we're new to kissing each other.'

'I think we…we fooled them at lunchtime.'

'Practice makes perfect,' he said. His heart pounded.

All he could think about was how much he wanted to kiss her. Ana.

He could see in her eyes she wanted to kiss him too.

His gaze dropped to her mouth, her lovely pink mouth with the generous lips that made him ache to taste them. He dipped his head. She rose up on her toes to meet him, putting her hands on his shoulders to balance. His mouth touched her lips for just a fleeting moment. He couldn't really call it a kiss. It was just the merest brushing of her lips to his before she broke the contact and pushed him away.

She stepped back. Crossed her arms over her chest. Her cheeks were flushed and her eyes glittered. 'We…we don't need to do this. This… this kind of kissing is dangerous. We don't need to practise. We've each kissed other people and know what to do.'

But they hadn't been Ana.

'I want to kiss you.'

'You do now. It's just proximity, Connor. If someone like Brandi were nearby, you wouldn't be wanting to kiss me. Not for real, that is.'

'That's not true.'

'I think you'll find it is. I'm not your type.'

He frowned. 'I don't have a type.'

'Please. Don't you? Think back to your girl-friends. All tall. Curvy. Blonde mainly. A couple of redheads.'

It was true. Yet why did he think petite with black hair and blue eyes was more his type? If he had to have a type, that is. Because he'd never let himself acknowledge it.

Because he didn't want to risk losing her. He'd put barriers up against being anything more than friends when they were teenagers because he hadn't been ready. Now they'd plunged headfirst into a fake marriage to complicate this…this stirring of attraction.

He went to get his clothes, still reeling at how Ana had pushed him away.

'Connor?' she called after him. She looked at him with a teasing smile. 'I promise not to peek.'

Ana was pleased that the conversation over dinner with Rose, Eve and Nate started by them admiring the bracelet she was wearing. It was a gold chain bracelet hung with a sliced piece of amethyst in a gold bezel setting.

'Is this from your online store?' Eve asked.

'It might be. Or I might keep it exclusive.'

'Did you make it yourself?' asked Rose.

'I didn't actually make the bracelet myself. I had it made by one of our external workshops. Then I added the amethyst, which is one of my favourite semi-precious gemstones.'

'I believe your store is very successful,' said Nate.

'It started small but, fingers crossed, it's growing,' she said. 'I'm an accountant by trade.' Not for much longer, she hoped. 'But I've always been interested in creative stuff.'

'Creative accounting can be a thing,' Connor said, and they all laughed.

'My great uncle Istvan in Budapest is a jeweller. When I visited as a teenager, he let me spend time in his workshop with him. I was hooked. Under his tutelage, I grew to see jewellery as wearable art. To please my family, I studied accountancy. But my heart has never been in it. I studied part-time to qualify in jewellery design and gemology.'

'When did you start the store?' said Rose.

'I met my business partner and dear friend, Kartika, at uni. We're so like-minded. She's Indonesian. On holiday with her in Bali one time, we met up with a community of artisan jewellery makers she knew. We started to sell some of their designs online. Then we commissioned that group to hand-make jewellery to our designs as well. We specialised in original but affordable designs that are just that bit different. It grew from there. We got a real boost when a Hollywood celebrity posted our earrings on social media. We now have our designs made in Jaipur, too. We're looking to source certain items worldwide—to sell worldwide, too, of course. A percentage of our profits goes to women's health projects in the countries where we source from.'

'How exciting,' said Eve. 'I'm very proud of you.'

'Thank you.' It meant so much to hear those words from these sisters who had been kept from her for so long.

"I really love your bracelet," said Eve.

'Me too. You're so talented,' said Rose.

Ana looked at Connor with a questioning raise of her eyebrows. He answered with a nod.

'I'm so glad you said that,' she said. 'Because I've made a bracelet for each of you and for Tilly.'

'You haven't!' said Eve.

'I was planning to give them to you for Christmas. I've got them with me. You can either wait to unwrap them on Christmas Day or—'

'We can unwrap them now,' said Rose.

'Yes, please,' said Eve.

Ana rose from her seat. 'They're in my room. I'll go get them.'

'You stay,' said Connor. 'I know where they are.'

As soon as Connor left the room, Eve leaned over the table. 'Connor is gorgeous. We approve.'

'He is rather wonderful,' said Ana. No need for creative fibs there.

'And fantastic with the horses,' said Rose. 'What an asset to Garrison Downs. Thank you for bringing him into the family.'

'Does he have his own veterinary practice?' asked Nate.

Ana shook her head. 'That's not what he wants. He's independently wealthy and wants to use his vet skills where he's needed as a volunteer.'

'That's so admirable,' said Rose.

Ana smiled. 'He's admirable all round.' Again, no need to lie.

'Not to mention hot,' said Eve. 'Was there ever anything more between you when you were younger?'

Ana could feel the blush warming her cheeks as she remembered that one, passionate kiss. 'No,' she said. 'We were just friends.'

'And yet, you've fallen for him now. What's changed, do you think?' said Eve.

Ana shrugged. She and Connor had anticipated this question. 'We spent six months apart. I think we both changed in that time. We… well…how can I explain falling in love? There's no reason to it.'

Eve exchanged a lingering glance with Nate. Ana saw the real love in their eyes. She was happy for her sister. Would she ever find love herself? Her mother was right. She'd never before come close to it.

'Are you two getting married so soon because of the will?' asked Rose.

'The short answer is yes,' said Ana. 'We might have waited longer for the actual wedding otherwise. But we both felt there was no point in waiting when so much is riding on us all getting married.'

An uncomfortable silence fell over the table. Ana didn't dare look at Rose. There was so much pressure on her older sister now.

Rose broke the silence. 'We're not going to lose the station,' she said. 'I promise.'

Just then, Connor arrived with three small parcels, exquisitely wrapped. 'Shall I be Santa and hand them out?' he said.

'Why not?' said Ana. Had she ever seen a Santa as good-looking as Connor? Even in a baggy red suit with a pillow down his front and a fake white beard, she'd want to climb onto his lap.

She waited until he put two of the parcels in front of Eve and Rose. 'I call these "the sister bracelets". That's the name I'll give them if we launch them in the store.' The gold in the four bracelets was of a much higher carat than used in most of their jewellery in the store. To keep prices reasonable, some pieces were gold-plated. Sterling-silver pieces were their best sellers.

'Can I go first?' asked Eve, eyeing her package with delight. 'Pretty please?'

'Before you open it, may I explain my choice of gemstones?' Ana said. 'All gemstones have a meaning, intrinsic to their qualities. Some people believe they can heal.' She held up her wrist. 'Purple amethyst is supposed to calm the emotions and encourage clarity of thought. But I just love the colour.'

Eve ripped open the paper to unwrap her gift. The bracelet was identical to Ana's, with its round gold links, but with a pure, pale semi-precious green stone. 'It's beautiful, Ana. I love it. Thank you!' Nate helped her fasten it on her wrist. She held her hand out for the others to see.

'The gem is amazonite,' said Ana. 'It's known as the gambler's stone, and is believed to bring good luck and success to those who wear it.'

Eve laughed. 'I wonder if our ancestor Louisa May, who won Garrison Downs in that poker game, was wearing amazonite at the time.' She blew a kiss across the table to Ana. 'I shall cherish my sister bracelet. Thank you.' She turned to her other sister. 'What's your stone, Rose?'

Rose unwrapped her parcel methodically. She stilled when she saw what was in it, swallowed and fastened her bracelet on her wrist. She held it up for the others to admire. Her gemstone was burnished golden with dark stripes.

'It's called tiger's eye,' said Ana. 'The gem promotes confidence and courage and helps keep balance and strength. I think you have those in spades, Rose.'

'So thoughtful of you,' Rose said. 'Thank you, Ana. This means a lot.'

'I love it too,' said Eve.

'The third parcel is for Matilda, right, Ana?' said Connor.

'Yes. I was going to post it to her and hope it got there in time for Christmas Day.'

'No need,' said Rose. 'Leave it with us to send over with our gifts. We get to use a diplomatic courier organised by Tilly.'

'Thank you.' Ana slid the parcel over to Rose.

'What gem did you choose for Tilly?' asked Eve.

'I debated over it but chose lapis lazuli. It's a beautiful blue. Fitting for a princess.'

'What are its qualities?' asked Eve.

'Lapis is said to promote wisdom and awareness, as well as to bring harmony to relationships,' Ana said. 'She might need that to be co-ruler of Chaleur.'

'A wise choice, Ana,' said Eve.

'Matilda chose such a different path to her sisters,' said Connor.

'I think love chose that path for her,' said Ana.

'Too right,' said Rose. 'And if anyone can make a success as a princess of an ancient principality, it's our Tilly alongside Henri.'

They decided to make a toast to Tilly. 'To absent princesses,' said Eve, holding up her glass.

'To Outback princesses present in this room,' said Connor, to Ana's surprise. He really did fit in here. He made the toast in mineral water. No wine for him, as he was piloting a plane the next day.

'Except I don't think I really qualify as an Outback princess,' Ana said in a small voice. 'City Cinderella, more like.'

Rose turned to her. 'You absolutely are one of us and don't ever think anything different. You have a blood connection here. One day you'll feel a heart connection to the land too.'

After the toast, Ana asked Connor to take some photos of the three sisters with their hands overlapping and their bracelets on show. There were lots of laughs before they got it right.

'Would you mind if I put this photo on the website if we launch this product? No identifying details, of course.'

'Absolutely,' said Rose.

'Shall we share these photos with Tilly?' Ana asked. 'If we do, it would ruin the surprise of her gift from me, as we'd have to tell her about ours.'

'Let's keep it a surprise,' said Eve. 'Rose and I will be here for Christmas, you'll be in Melbourne with your family and she'll be in a foreign country.'

'It's not foreign to her now,' said Nate. 'Chaleur is her home. She has responsibilities that will keep her there.'

'Nevertheless, these bracelets will be a way to unite us, wherever we may be,' said Eve. 'I'll always think of my sisters when I wear mine.'

'Me too,' Ana said at the same time as Rose.

Ana was so tired by the time she and Connor got back to the yellow suite, she wouldn't let him argue about who was getting the bed. It was all she could do to summon the energy to get into her pyjamas. 'This is my house—or it will be—and I say I'm taking the sofa. You'll need all your wits about you to pilot that plane tomorrow. Just toss me the extra pillows and I'll make myself snug with this throw, okay?'

She didn't make herself snug. The *chaise longue* was hard and uncomfortable. Ana suspected it was designed for looks rather than comfortable sitting, let alone sleeping. She didn't know what time it was when she finally admitted defeat and sneaked into the big, divinely comfortable bed. Trying not to disturb a slumbering Connor, she tucked herself in on the edge of the bed as far as she could be away from him. But he stirred, opened his eyes, smiled a sleepy smile—though she wasn't sure if he was actually awake—and reached out a hand to her across the expanse of crisp, white sheet. She reached out her own hand and let him fold it into his. She couldn't help an answering smile before she went to sleep, holding Connor's hand, feeling blissfully happy and secure.

When she awoke to the morning sun streaming through the shutters, the bed was empty, the sheets rumpled on Connor's side of the bed. She could hear him in the shower. Had she really been holding hands with Connor all night?

She dismissed it as a dream.

CHAPTER EIGHT

ANA KNEW HER mother and grandparents would be happy about her engagement to Connor. But she hadn't anticipated just how happy. She hadn't expected her grandmother to burst into tears of joy when she and Connor announced their news on their return from Garrison Downs. Or her grandfather to be quite so proud and excited at the prospect of his granddaughter's wedding. Everybody loved Connor. And they loved the idea of Ana and Connor as a couple.

Her grandmother had immediately demanded to know if the hastily planned wedding was because Ana was pregnant. But Nagymama didn't care if she was. Because Connor was the father, and they loved Connor and knew he would do the right thing by marrying her. In fact, Nagymama seemed disappointed when Ana told her she wasn't pregnant. 'I hope you won't wait too long before giving us a great-grandchild,' she'd said. What a difference a wedding ring made.

Only her mother had pulled her aside to gently ask if she was sure, that this had happened very quickly.

'I've known Connor for most of my life, Mum,' she'd said. 'You can hardly say we don't know each other.'

'You know each other as friends, not as lovers,' her mother had said.

'I know the difference, Mum.'

If only she did!

Since the trip to Garrison Downs there had only been affectionate kisses on the cheek, some hand-holding and the odd arm around her shoulders. All in the interests of appearing to be a happily engaged couple in front of other people. Nothing like the heat of that almost-kiss moment in the privacy of their shared bedroom in the yellow suite.

The fact that soon into the new year Connor had been called away to an animal rescue on the other side of the country was fortuitous. Her wanting him for real was becoming like an obsession—one she had to hide from him. Yet other people expected her to be obsessed with Connor. After all, they were getting married.

'Yes, I miss him. Of course I miss him. Yes, I can't wait for him to be back.' She'd said all that, acting the lonely fiancée, and meaning it. She did miss him. Every day, in fact. But, in a way, she was relieved. The more time she spent with him, the more she found it difficult to fight that growing attraction.

It was as if she was looking at him differently from how she had ever done. And liking that new Connor way too much. Because although Connor had wanted to kiss her—seriously kiss her—it had not been in the context of anything deeper. Friends with benefits. Was that the way he saw it happening between them while they were forced into proximity? Or was it just because they were both available? What had he said about how a guy would say anything he thought a girl wanted to hear to get her into bed?

'If you're sure this is the right thing for you both, I'm very happy for you and Connor,' her mother had said. 'I couldn't ask for a better son-in-law. And, of course, you getting married will help fulfil that archaic requirement of your father's will. Your sisters must be very pleased. Only Rose to go now, isn't it?'

There wasn't a moment when Ana didn't feel bad about deceiving her family. But it had to be done. They couldn't risk there being any legal implication for the inheritance if their marriage was seen to be fake.

In the plane heading back to Melbourne after their visit to Garrison Downs, she had told Connor she would plan a simple, quiet wedding for the middle of January. Maybe in the registry office—they only needed two witnesses.

She should have realised that was never going to happen.

'Your grandparents would feel cheated, darling,' her mum had said. 'After all, I didn't ever have a wedding. Would I feel cheated too? Yes, I would. I want to see my daughter a bride. If you're getting married, let's do it properly.'

Ana had agreed to a 'proper' wedding. But what she wouldn't agree to was a religious ceremony. That would be just too hypocritical.

Before she knew it, the rest of December, Christmas and New Year had been pretty much taken up by wedding plans. She soon discovered that planning a wedding at a month's notice wasn't that simple. Wedding venues booked out sometimes years ahead. So did celebrants, florists, caterers and cake-makers. And custom-made wedding dresses needed to be ordered up to six months in advance.

But the community Ana's family had lived in since her grandparents came to Australia pulled together to help Dori and Zoltan's granddaughter get married in style. It soon became apparent there could be no other choice of venue—her grandparents' restaurant, where she and Connor had spent such happy times over the years and was like a second home. The restaurant was closed on Mondays and Tuesdays. That made a Tuesday the ideal day for Nagypapa and Nagymama to host the wedding. A week day also made sense, as wedding suppliers were booked out for weekends in January.

Everything started to fall into place. A friend of a regular customer had a friend who had a friend who had just qualified as a marriage celebrant. One of Nagymama's friends owned a wonderful St Kilda cake shop and wanted to gift them a wedding cake. Lili's florist friend insisted she do the flowers.

Ana found the perfect dress in a sample sale at one of Melbourne's best wedding designers. It was nineteen-fifties-inspired in ivory silk, full-skirted, tea-length, off the shoulders and laced down the back. And she loved it. She couldn't resist a short veil, retro and perfect. After all, would she ever dress as a bride again? Kartika, her bridesmaid, was bringing a beautiful soft blue dress in a similar style with her from Jakarta.

If it was a real wedding, of course Ana would want her sisters to be bridesmaids too. That would be a dream come true. But it wasn't possible anyway, because the sisters were still keeping their relationship secret. Rose and Eve would, however, be at the wedding as guests.

Tilly had been in tears when she'd explained why she couldn't be there. There were royal occasions in Chaleur at which she simply had to be present. To be away in Australia would be a breach of royal protocol the newly minted Princess Matilda simply couldn't make.

Ana had made the wedding bands herself, thinking all the time she could melt them down after the marriage was dissolved. She could perhaps make earrings with the salvaged gold and platinum. But would she ever have the heart to wear them?

All Connor had to do was get suits for him and his brother Billy, who was his best man. It turned out Connor had a suit he'd never worn, a wheat-coloured linen three-piece he'd had tailor-made in Hoi An on a vacation to Vietnam. Perfect.

Her best friend would be the best dressed, most handsome hire-a-husband Melbourne had ever seen.

In the lead up to the wedding, Connor found himself strangely edgy. On more than one occasion, Ana had given him the chance to back down from their arrangement. There was no way he would do that. There was way too much at stake. And had the marriage of convenience—which he'd started to call the mock— not been his idea in the first place?

Fortunately—or unfortunately, as he found himself missing her every day he was away—he'd been called to an emergency rescue of sea birds caught in an oil spill in Western Australia. The number of pelicans with their feathers covered in oil and choking on it was tragic. He was grateful for the veterinary skills that enabled him to help save them.

That had taken him away from Melbourne from just after the new year to just a few days before the wedding. It was a relief in a way, because their sudden engagement after twenty years of just being friends had put the two of them under the microscope. And under a microscope was an uncomfortable place to be—especially when he and Ana had to be so careful not to tangle themselves up in the web of lies they were weaving around the wedding.

How many times had he fielded the question, 'Why get married in such a hurry? Is Ana pregnant?' As if it was anyone's business but their own if she was.

Not that there was any chance of Ana getting pregnant. There hadn't even been a kiss between them since they'd got back from Garrison Downs. But he'd thought about kissing her. A lot.

Now today was their wedding day. Their mock-wedding day, that is. Although the ceremony was totally legal, it was never going to be a real marriage. It seemed surreal that today he and Ana would officially become husband and wife in the eyes of the world. But, when he thought about the magnificence of Garrison Downs, he knew it was worth it. When he thought about Ana's anticipation at taking her jewellery business to the next level and beyond, he knew it was worth it. When he thought of how much she cherished her relationship with her sisters and the future they had planned as a family, he knew it was worth it.

Fortunately, he knew the major players in this wedding well. Not one person had expressed anything but happiness that he and Ana, best friends for so long, were getting married. Her mother. Her grandparents. Kartika, who had flown down from Indonesia two days ago. His parents—his mother here with her second husband, his father with his latest girlfriend—were as delighted as Ana's family. As his mother had said, 'Finally, you've recognised what has been under your nose for so long. Ana is the one for you.'

It wouldn't be easy to face them when he and Ana engineered a divorce. Their 'breakup' would hurt and disappoint the people closest to them. That wasn't something he'd thought about when he'd come up with the idea for the mock marriage.

It was late afternoon and the clock was ticking for Ana to come downstairs from where she was getting ready with Kartika in her grandparents' flat above the restaurant. The restaurant had been transformed with swathes of airy white fabric, fairy lights and masses of beautiful flowers in pastel shades. Girly? Yes, but that was Ana, and it seemed just right both for the room and the occasion.

It was…romantic. Even he couldn't fail to recognise that. An area towards the back of the restaurant had been chosen for the ceremony to take place. He and Ana would make their vows under an arch that had been completely covered in fresh, pale-pink roses.

A guitarist strummed quietly as the guests gathered. There were more than thirty guests in the restaurant waiting, with him, for their first sight of the bride. The guests were a mix of family and close friends. Only one of his Money Club partners had been able to make the wedding at such short notice—Adrian Chong and his delightful wife Chloe had flown down from their home in Singapore.

Two out of three of Ana's sisters were there. It was Matilda's first winter as a princess of Chaleur and she had no way of getting out of her traditional role of presiding over the winter festival—a very big deal in that small principality. She had sent an extravagant gift, plus an elegantly hand-scripted note of loving good wishes on embossed paper headed with her royal coat of arms.

Connor chatted with Eve, Nate and Rose. He noted the sisters were wearing their sister bracelets, and he knew Ana planned to wear hers. None of the other guests knew Ana's sisters. They were part of that web of secrecy regarding her father that still enmeshed Ana. He let the other guests assume the sisters were university friends.

The door to upstairs opened. Ana's grandfather asked people to take their places and to clear the makeshift aisle between the tables as the bride would soon be arriving. He and Billy, in a deep-blue linen suit, took their places at the side of the rose arch. Connor was nervous, cracking the knuckles of his left hand, until Billy hissed at him to stop. Kartika came through the door first, lovely in a powder-blue dress, smiling at him. Something in her smile made him wonder if Ana had confided in her the truth about the wedding.

Then he saw Ana. Ana looking ethereally beautiful in a white dress he was seeing for the first time, as tradition dictated. And he had eyes for no one else. Ana, like he'd never seen her before.

His bride.

She was a bride A full-on, traditional bride. Ana marvelled at how she'd got here. She'd tried so hard to keep it simple, because the wedding wasn't for real. But no one else but she and Connor, and now Kartika, knew that. So she'd succumbed to the pressure from her family and got swept up in the glamour and fun of it. So here she was in her dream dress, the skirt held out with layers of stiff, retro petticoats, her face covered by the cute, chin-length veil and wearing high-heeled, peep-toe white pumps. 'You look like Audrey Hepburn,' Kartika had said after she'd finished her bridesmaid's work of helping the bride get dressed in her finery.

Now Ana stepped her way down the short aisle towards her husband-to-be.

As she got closer, she could tell Connor was as nervous as she was. They were in this fraud together. Each only too aware of what could be at stake if they were exposed. She glanced around her to see the smiling faces of people who cared about her. She knew they wished her a lifetime of happiness with Connor. She felt a distinct twinge of guilt at the deception. Then she caught Rose's eye and remembered exactly why they were doing this.

Rose and Ana subtly raised their hands to show they were wearing their sister bracelets. Ana was clutching her hand-tied bouquet of roses and eucalypt leaves, so couldn't risk a wave back in return in case she dropped it. But she could tell her sisters saw she was wearing her bracelet over the long white gloves her wedding dress had called for. Her other jewellery comprised a two-strand choker of baroque white pearls, and the pearl earrings her mother had given her for her twenty-first birthday. And, of course, that elaborate engagement ring.

Connor looked exceedingly handsome. She was so proud of him. Of everything he'd achieved. Of what a good person he was. If the look in his eyes was anything to go by, he admired the way she looked too. And that look made her feel beautiful. He had always made her feel good about herself, way back to those days in primary school when he'd protected her from bullies. Or when he'd assured her that the braces she'd had to wear on her teeth for a year when she'd been twelve looked cute. She felt a rush of affection and gratitude towards him that swelled her heart.

This really was a wonderful occasion, surrounded by well-wishers, a superb meal to come and music for dancing. A celebratory party. That's how she should think about it to wash away the guilt of their deception. To think it could ever be anything else could only lead to heartbreak. She knew she was in danger of falling in love with her old friend, and she simply couldn't allow it to happen. Not if she wanted to keep him in her life when it was all over.

She neared the rose arch where Connor waited for her. He was either as overwhelmed as she was by the waves of goodwill in the room, or a darn good actor, because his affection for her shone from his gaze. That look made her heart feel quite fluttery, as if it were accelerating a beat or two—not a feeling that proximity to Connor usually evoked. Not until recently, anyway.

Ana handed her bouquet to Kartika and let her bridesmaid help her slide off the long white gloves. Kartika then took her place next to Billy. Ana took the few steps that would take her very close to Connor. Then she lifted the wisp of a veil back from her face. Offering herself in marriage to her man. According to wedding etiquette, her father should have done that after he'd walked her up the aisle. She felt a surge of sadness that Holt was not with her. Not that he could have been acknowledged as the father of the bride. But she banished that sadness in the warmth and admiration of Connor's smile.

To the delight of their guests, she walked into his arms. She stood on tip toe to nuzzle into his neck, her lips on his warm, smooth skin, and murmured so no one else could hear. 'I know this must seem ridiculous. You probably want to laugh. The way I'm dealing with it is to pretend that this gathering is a celebration of our friendship. Twenty years of friendship and caring—it really is something to celebrate. Let's relax and enjoy it without worrying about what might come next.'

She felt Connor relax, and he smiled that familiar Connor smile. 'Great idea,' he whispered. 'You always know what to do.'

'Let's get you two married,' said the celebrant, a charming, articulate young woman.

Ana felt like a spell had been cast over her as she repeated her wedding vows to Connor, framed by the rose arch. He seemed to be under the same spell as he confidently spoke the vows in his clear deep voice, sounding sincere and convincing. No one would believe this wasn't for real. She had to make sure *she* realised it wasn't for real. Because when Connor looked into her eyes and said, 'Anastasia Katherine Horvath, I take you to be my lawful, wedded wife,' she found herself thrilling to the illicit idea of what it would be like to be in a real relationship with Connor. She noticed his hands weren't quite steady as he slid the wedding band onto the third finger of her left hand, above the elaborate engagement ring that was as fake as the vows they'd just exchanged.

What would it be like if they were for real?

It seemed only moments before the celebrant intoned, 'I now pronounce you man and wife. Mr and Mrs Connor O'Neill.' Their guests started to clap and applaud.

But Ana startled at those words. Through all the time spent preparing for the wedding, she hadn't even thought that people might call her Mrs O'Neill. Surely she wouldn't be expected to change her name? That would bring all sorts of complications.

It brought to front of mind the reasons why she didn't want to get married—married for real, that was. For so long, she had fulfilled the expectations of her family when it came to her career. She had undergone this fake marriage to gain her inheritance. That inheritance would give her the means to soar free to follow her own interests. To grow her business. To travel. To answer to no one but herself. Certainly not to a husband. A man who might expect her to take his name. And who might clip her wings.

The celebrant continued. 'Connor, you may kiss your bride.'

Ana looked up at Connor, smile set in place, expecting a sweet kiss on the cheek.

Instead, Connor took her by surprise by wrapping his arms around her, pulling her in close and bending her back into the classic bride swoop. Then he kissed her, firmly on the mouth. To all intents and purposes, he was claiming his woman. *Well played, Connor.*

There were cheers and more clapping from their guests. But Ana was oblivious to the rejoicing, too intoxicated by Connor's closeness. By Connor's mouth on hers, his arms tight around her, his warmth, his strength, the familiar scent of him. She kissed him back, wanting more, wanting *him*. He swooped her back upright without breaking the kiss. She wound her arms around his neck, pulling him closer, deepening the kiss, caressing the seam of his mouth with the tip of her tongue, feeling his in return, not wanting it to end. She could tell herself that, conscious of an audience, she was only kissing him in such an exaggerated manner to emphasise the genuine nature of the marriage. But she knew she was kidding herself.

Her only thought was to be closer to him.

She was kissing Connor for real.

'Woo-hoo!' called several guests.

'Get a room, you two. You're married now!' called another.

Ana broke away from the kiss, flushed and laughing. But she didn't take her eyes from Connor's. Because for one long, exhilarating moment she saw in his green gaze the same mix of surprise, awareness and desire that she was sure he could see in hers.

That look gave her hope that perhaps something more might come of this. Maybe even a negotiated friends with benefits scenario. She wanted more than kisses from Connor. But she wasn't sure how to get there. Not when they'd tied themselves up in so many conditions relating to the mock marriage. Not with that long history of hands-off, platonic friendship—a friendship she didn't want to risk losing.

Within seconds, she and Connor were swept up in congratulations and hugs. The tearful embrace of them both by her mother. 'My new son!' she said, through happy tears. 'I couldn't be more pleased.'

There were more, 'Congratulations, Mrs O'Neill!' than Ana could keep count of.

Then there was the sit-down meal, featuring their Hungarian favourites. A few mercifully brief speeches. The cutting of the magnificent two-tier cake adorned with roses. Dancing. And then the evening was over.

They'd done it. She and Connor had pulled it off.

They were married.

There was one more traditional touch to the celebrations. The tossing of the bride's bouquet. Whoever caught it would be the next to be married. Ana stood with her back to the group of single ladies then tossed her bouquet backwards over her shoulder. When she turned round, it was to find it had been caught by Rose, who stood holding it awkwardly in front of her. Ana could see the startled surprise in Rose's blue Waverly eyes. And something else passed between her, Rose and Eve. Hope.

Three sisters wed and one to go.

Ana had resisted the idea of a honeymoon. But Connor had pointed out that he needed a holiday, so did she, and that it would seem odd if they each returned to their separate homes the day after the wedding. Her grandfather had apparently taken Connor aside after they'd announced their engagement and suggested they honeymoon in Budapest—and had offered to pay for it. Connor told her he had thanked him but insisted on paying for everything. With no contribution from Ana either. He could well afford it and would brook no arguments, he'd said, over her protests. Budapest. There was nowhere else she'd rather go. Then Connor had thrown in the extra surprise of a visit to Matilda and Henri in Chaleur on the way home.

They left the reception in an elegant, chauffeured vintage car, organised by Connor as a surprise, and headed to an airport hotel where they could crash for the remaining hours of the night before taking a very early flight to Hungary.

Two weeks alone with Connor. Who knew what might happen? She had pushed him away in that yellow suite at Garrison Downs. Maybe next time they shared a room she might have to let him know how much she wanted him. How much she was prepared to risk taking their relationship to the next step.

She might have to convince him to seduce her.

Connor sat in the back of the vintage 1964 Rolls-Royce Silver Cloud, headed to the airport hotel. The guests had cheered when the very stylish vehicle had pulled up in front of the restaurant. Ana had laughed in delight. She'd been expecting the standard limo, but he'd wanted to surprise her. He'd known the car would appeal to her love of vintage. It was his contribution to a wedding where she'd done most of the work. He kept casting glances at her, sitting beside him on the luxurious leather seat. She was still in her wedding dress, although the sassy little veil and the sexy gloves had come off for dancing.

Ana, his childhood friend, was now his wife. He had mixed feelings about it. Foremost, he was glad he was able to help her attain her inheritance. But the shared vows of the ceremony had triggered a shift in his feelings about marriage that was percolating through his thoughts.

She yawned. 'Didn't it go off well? Such a good party. And we played our roles brilliantly, didn't we?'

'We did,' he said.

Was it still just a role for her? The thought was disconcerting. Because during the ceremony he'd found himself so involved in his role of pretend husband, he'd started to believe in the possibility of a marriage with Ana. When he'd slipped that platinum ring on her finger, he'd felt he was securing her as his wife. It had seemed so real and somehow so *right*. And as for that kiss… He'd started it as something playful, but very quickly it had become something altogether more passionate. The more he thought about that kiss, about those heartfelt vows, the more possible it seemed. Ana. Him. Married. For real.

Obviously exhausted, Ana yawned again and put her hand over her mouth. For weeks, she'd worked so hard to get the make-believe wedding organised. It had gone off flawlessly. 'Sorry,' she said. 'So tired. I didn't get much sleep the past few nights.'

Without a word, he pulled her to him. With a sigh, she nestled her head against his shoulder, her soft hair brushing across his neck. Within seconds her breathing changed and he knew she was asleep. Connor inhaled her sweet, warm, familiar scent.

He felt an immense wave of tenderness for her. Fate hadn't dealt his friend the easiest of hands with the way she'd had to exist under the cloud of secrets and lies surrounding her birth. Never able to tell anyone that she had a living father, let alone who he was.

Yet she'd never complained. Even though he knew how heartbroken she'd been every time her father had left after one of his fleeting visits. He knew she would have thought about Holt today, although not a mention had been made of the father of the bride. Yet in the wording of his will Holt had shown how much he had cared for her—and bequeathed Ana her three sisters. The acknowledgment by her Waverly family had made a difference to her.

To ensure she got what her father had wanted for all his daughters, Connor had stepped up. He hadn't regretted it for a second. Never had

Connor felt more protective of her. Not just protective. Possessive. With his right arm around her, his other hand lay on his knee. In the darkness of the opulent car interior, the brand-new gold wedding band on the third finger of his left hand gleamed. In the eyes of the world, he was married. It didn't feel as weird as he'd thought it would.

As Ana snuggled in against him, Connor thought about his long friendship with her. How important she was to him. How much he'd missed her when he'd been working away with the pelicans before the wedding. How he felt more at ease with her than with any other woman—in fact, with any other person. Ana Horvath was, when he really thought about it, his favourite person. Smart, kind, funny, unstintingly loyal. What a huge, horrible hole would be left be in his life without her.

There was also the not insignificant fact that he desired her. Was becoming obsessed with wanting to bed her. Rather than thoughts of stepping back from crossing the friendship line, his mind was flooded with thoughts of galloping across it.

She had never looked more beautiful than today. He wanted her so badly, it had showed in the hunger in his eyes as he'd watched her chat with their guests. Or so both his brother and Adrian had informed him. Then relent-lessly teased him about it. But that was okay. He and Ana were married. People expected him to be passionate about his bride at their wedding. Expected that kind of teasing about their wedding night. Ana would no doubt put his reaction down to his good acting. But he hadn't been acting.

He thought about what his mother had said at the announcement of their engagement. 'Finally you've recognised what has been under your nose for so long. Ana is the one for you.'

Was there any truth in his mother's words? Could it be that the other women he'd dated had fallen short when compared to Ana? Was that why they'd never lasted? He feared marriage. But his anti-marriage stance rested mainly on a platform of distrust. Ana had never given him cause not to trust her. She hated the deception she'd grown up having to tolerate. Would he trust himself to be faithful to her? For the first time ever, he thought he needed to consider the fact that marriage to Ana fell in a completely different basket than marriage to anybody else.

Their luggage for the honeymoon had been sent ahead to the hotel. All they had to do was check in when they arrived. He gently awakened Ana from where she was sleeping on his shoulder. Startled and still half asleep, she looked up at him, then smiled a slow, warm smile of recognition that sent tingles down his spine. She had never before looked at him like that.

'You,' she said sleepily, a wealth of emotion shining from her eyes. 'It's you.' Then she blinked, shook her head and pulled back from him. 'Sorry. I… I was dreaming. But I can't remember…'

Dreaming of him? If yes, he hoped it had not just been a happy dream but possibly an erotic one. He stilled. What if she'd been dreaming about another man? He felt shocked by the jealousy that knifed through him.

Extra solicitously, he helped her out of the car, to be greeted by the steamy January night air. 'Hard to believe we'll be in winter tomorrow,' he said. A mundane comment to disguise the tumult of his thoughts. Not at all what he'd really like to say to her.

'I can't wait,' she said. 'I love Budapest. I'm sure you will too.'

Ana had booked the airport hotel room. Connor wasn't surprised to see there were twin beds. He remembered the fuss she'd made about a bed at Garrison Downs. She should be very pleased with the Budapest hotel he had booked.

Ana staggered into the room ahead of him, exaggerating each step. 'I only had two flutes of champagne,' she said. 'I'm walking like this because my shoes are killing me. They're new and I didn't have time to wear them in.'

He smiled. Still the same Ana. She'd developed a taste for shoes that looked so uncomfortable he didn't know how anyone could wear them. But she always looked fantastic in them.

She threw herself back onto one of the beds and kicked off her shoes. 'We only have a few hours here before we need to be at the airport. It's hardly worth getting undressed.'

'So you'd get on the plane in your wedding dress? Could be uncomfortable.'

'You're right,' she said with a sigh, sitting up on the bed. 'But, Connor, I can't get out of this dress by myself.' She got up from the bed and turned her back to him. Looked over her shoulder with imploring blue eyes. 'See? It's tightly laced all the way down the back. The lady in the bridal shop said a zipper was simply not romantic for a wedding gown.'

Connor had noticed. He had noticed the way the silk laces crisscrossed her body, cinching in her already narrow waist. She was all wrapped up in that dress, like a beautiful gift just crying out to be unwrapped. Romantic, perhaps. Sexy as hell, yes.

During the reception, the thought had crossed his mind about how it might be to undo those laces. To watch that dress slide off her shoulders down her body to pool in a froth of white on the floor. In his fantasies, she had stepped out of the dress wearing only those sexy, high-heeled shoes. She might even had smiled a sensual, come-and-get-me smile. More than once, that fantasy had played across his mind.

'Kartika had to tightly lace me into the dress,' Ana said.

Connor had to clear his throat. 'Now you're asking me to unlace you out of it?' he said hoarsely.

'Yes. Please. If you don't mind.'

He gritted his teeth. This prosaic request was hardly what he had been fantasising about all evening. 'I suppose I must,' he said, more grumpily than he had intended. How would he be able to hold back from distinctly un-friend-like behaviour when she was inviting him to undress her? If this were anyone but Ana, he might think she was teasing him.

He forced himself to stand behind her and calmly loosen the laces that crisscrossed her back, then pull them open. Her skin was smooth and warm under his hands. Did her breath quicken at his touch? Or was that wishful thinking? The dress started to slide down her shoulders and off her body, revealing the creamy skin of her back. The front of the dress loosened too.

Ana clutched the fabric to her chest. She wasn't wearing a bra and the curves of her breasts were tantalisingly revealed. Were her nipples peaking at his gaze? Connor valiantly fought the temptation to slide his hands over her shoulders and down the sides of her breasts. To push the dress over her hips. Was she wearing panties?

She turned to face him. Her face was flushed, her eyes dilated. 'Thank you. I… I can manage now.'

'Are you sure you don't need any further help?' he said through gritted teeth.

'Quite sure,' she said. Her tone wasn't as certain as her words suggested.

He couldn't stay here, with her in that alluring state of semi-undress, for a moment longer. He stepped back. 'I'll go shower while you change.'

'Good idea,' she said, still clutching the dress to herself to preserve her modesty. The action pushed her breasts upward in a most enticing way but she seemed oblivious to it. He, who knew her so well, couldn't detect even a touch of regret in those beautiful Waverly blue eyes. Let alone any hint of desire. Certainly not the kind of high-level lust he was feeling. He'd obviously read more into her response to his swooping kiss at the wedding than had actually been there.

After his shower, he stepped back into the room to find Ana fast asleep on the bed, wrapped in the white towelling robe provided by the hotel. She slept with her cheek resting on her hand. Her make-up was smudged dark around her eyes. She looked vulnerable and alone. He pulled the cover up over her, as the air conditioning was quite chilly.

So much for any ideas about a real wedding night.

He slipped into the other bed. But he couldn't sleep. Two weeks alone with Ana in Budapest. What had he let himself in for?

CHAPTER NINE

Seducing Connor into seducing her was top of Ana's wish list for their Budapest 'honeymoon'. She'd wimped out back in the Melbourne airport hotel, too exhausted to do anything about her desire to lure him into bed. Just as well, really, as they'd only had a few hours before their flight left Melbourne. It could have been excruciatingly awkward.

However, once in Budapest, her secret hopes that he might have the same agenda for the honeymoon were dashed on their arrival in the glorious city of her ancestors. Her generous husband-in-name-only had booked them into a fabulous five-star hotel in a grand, historic building overlooking the River Danube. In a luxury suite with two separate bedrooms and two bells-and-whistles marble bathrooms.

'No need for either of us to have to sleep on the sofa,' Connor explained.

'Or squabble over bathroom time,' she agreed, trying to sound cheerful.

There went the 'only one bed' scenario for seduction. Darn Connor for being so thoughtful. But he was working on out-of-date information concerning her attitude about sharing a bed with him.

'I thought you'd be pleased,' he said, sounding rather pleased with himself in his own gruff way.

Not, she thought. 'Of course,' she said through gritted teeth.

Now was her chance to say she would have been more than happy to sleep in the bed with him. However, perhaps it wasn't quite the right moment. Not when she'd made such a fuss of sleeping on the back-breaking sofa back at Garrison Downs. But that had been before the wedding. Before that exhilarating kiss when she'd thought, for the first time, he might want her too. Before the exciting touch of his hands on her bare skin as he'd unlaced her wedding dress.

Had that affected him at all? And did he remember holding her hand as she'd fallen asleep, in that big bed in the yellow suite at Garrison Downs before Christmas? Perhaps she had dreamed it, but it had seemed so real at the time. She couldn't forget how blissfully happy the contact had made her. She'd been hoping, somehow, to recreate it. And more.

Anyway, what was the big fuss about making love in a bed? There was the sofa, the carpet, up against the wall; even the bath tub, for heaven's sake. If she got the chance to get physical with Connor, she wouldn't care about the comfort factor of a hotel bed.

They'd just arrived after the very long, but exceedingly comfortable, first-class flight from Melbourne via Dubai. She hadn't flown first class before and it had been a revelation. Gourmet meals, an on-board spa, even a bar serving drinks in a first-class lounge. Utterly exhausted after the wedding, she'd slept for a lot of the trip, in the first-class pyjamas, on the flat bed made up with crisp sheets. *Thank you, Connor, for your generosity.* She'd nearly fainted when she'd seen how much the fares had cost.

Now she did a twirl in the ballroom-sized living area. 'This suite is amazing,' she said. 'Clever you for getting it for us. Thank you.'

'I thought you'd like it,' he said.

The room must have cost him another small fortune.

She walked over to the window and pulled the curtains further back so she could see the view in its entirety. She caught her breath. Snowflakes slowly drifted past, enhancing the already beautiful view of the famous Chain Bridge. The elegant, nineteenth-century bridge spanned the River Danube to connect the Pest side of the city, where their hotel was, to the Buda side. Across the river, a dusting of snow covered the Fisherman's Bastion and the Matthias Church with the elaborate spires and turrets. Places she wanted to visit.

'Budapest is even more beautiful than I remember,' she said. 'The buildings all frosted with snow make it look like something out of a fairy tale. I'm aching to get out there and show you what an awesome city it is.'

Connor joined her at the window. 'It's magnificent: the river; the old buildings; the snow. This is a world away from Garrison Downs Yet each place is spectacularly beautiful in its own way.'

Ana was very aware of him standing by her shoulder, his height and strength. He was wearing black jeans and boots and a lightweight black cashmere sweater. It wasn't his usual look and she found it incredibly attractive. Although they'd freshened up in the first-class lounge during a short layover in Dubai, he was sporting a sexy stubble. She liked that too. How would it feel against her cheek if she kissed him?

Again, she was struck by the realisation that,

in some ways, Connor was different. Had he changed so much in the six months he'd been away in Sydney? Or had she not noticed cumulative, ongoing changes in her childhood friend usually masked by everyday familiarity? Then, wham, she'd been hit by that change when she'd met him at the restaurant after a half-year absence. When she'd realised he was no longer the boy next door. Not a boy at all. A man.

A man she wanted.

If she'd wanted him as much then as she wanted him now, she didn't know how she could have maintained a platonic friendship through recent years. Now the fake intimacy they'd needed to cultivate for the sake of the wedding was accelerating those disturbing new feelings.

They were married.

It was almost as if that fact gave permission for something different to happen. Besides, didn't the marriage have to be consummated to be legal?

'What do you know about Budapest?' she asked as they both looked out at the view.

'Not a lot. I've chatted with your grandparents about the events that drove them to Australia. And I've heard from you about your visits here when you were younger. But there's much to learn.'

'For me, too,' she said.

He turned to look down into her face. His expression was serious.

Did he get more handsome by the minute?

'This is your heritage as much as Garrison Downs. The culture. The architecture. The music. They all speak to your Hungarian side. After all you've gone through with the shock of your father's death and the drama of the will, I wanted to bring you here. To restore some balance to your view of yourself.'

'Really?' She felt flooded with gratitude for his understanding. 'Thank you, Connor. That seems very profound and…and very perceptive. You know me so well. As if you haven't done enough for me by acting as my husband.'

She was going to add, 'What would I do without you?' But she didn't think it wise. Because those weeks when they hadn't communicated, because of her dislike of Brandi, had let her know exactly what it was like not to have Connor in her life. It had been awful, like a great, gaping hole in her heart. Yet, at the same time, might it be worth taking a risk to see if there could be more than friendship between them? Though, that hadn't worked out too well on their wedding night.

'You know I wanted to help with the mock.

Now there's a signed marriage certificate in hand,' he said.

The 'mock' was what he called the marriage of convenience.

Distancing himself, perhaps, with humour from their deception of so many people who cared for them. 'Your grandfather told me how much you wanted to come back here. He felt you needed it. We cooked this trip up together.'

Did she need it? Maybe she did, to have some distance. To overcome that nagging sense that she didn't really belong at Garrison Downs. That the place was all about Rosamund and her daughters, with the secret daughter banging at the back door to be let in. What had happened in the last seven months had been overwhelming at times. Apa's death and the terrible grief she'd felt at his loss. The complications of the will. The unproductive and demoralising hunt for a husband. The way her attraction to Connor had burst out of the boundaries she had put around it for so long.

'It's true what Nagypapa said. I've been saving for a trip for ages. My grandparents knew that. They've always encouraged me to feel connected to the family we have left here. This will be the third time I've visited but the first time I've been here by myself.'

'By yourself?' he said. 'I'm here, aren't I? Or are you planning to ditch me?'

She expected him to nudge her on the arm in his jocular, we-are-good-mates style, the way he had always done. But he didn't. He sounded light-hearted but the shadows in his green eyes said something else. Had she hurt his feelings? She couldn't bear it if she had. Who knew with all the play acting that had been going on between them in the interests of the mock marriage? Did she really know how Connor felt?

'Oh, Connor, I'm so sorry. That's not what I meant at all. I meant the first time I've travelled independently. I'm so grateful you're here with me. I wouldn't even be here if it wasn't for you.'

Now. She took a deep breath. Now she should say something about a change in direction for their friendship. *Now.* But she couldn't bring herself to say the words. 'I meant, the first time I was with my grandparents. The second time I was on the budget bus tour with my university friends.' And wishing he'd been there too, to share in the fun.

'In your second year. July holidays. I remember.'

'Yep. Eastern Europe in two weeks. We were only in Budapest for one night. Not nearly enough to sample all that there was to do here.

But the trip was a lot of fun. We all loved the ruin bars.'

'A ruin bar? A bar where you get ruined? Isn't that what students do anyway?'

She laughed. 'That, too.' Not her, though. She never allowed herself to get drunk. Not when she was sitting on that big secret of her birth. Wariness with strangers who wanted to get to know her had become second nature.

'Budapest ruin bars are cool bars that sprung up in dilapidated buildings, abandoned warehouses, ruins—even underground. They're mainly in the downtown Pest area. You know this side of the river is Pest, the other side is Buda?'

'I didn't know that. I do now. I'm up for visiting ruin bars,' he said. 'You'll have to be my guide.'

'I have some cousins our age here. I'm sure they could show us where the locals go.'

'And how to avoid tourist traps,' he said.

'That too. My first trips were in summer and autumn. But Budapest in winter is different altogether, and so beautiful.'

'Especially to Australian eyes, having come straight from summer.'

Leaving steamy, summer Melbourne to land here in the cold and snow was a shock to the senses. A shock of a very good kind. She loved it.

'I believe there's a big outdoor ice rink in the City Park,' she said. 'You've never ice-skated, have you?'

'No.'

'Didn't think so,' she said. 'Neither have I. Do you want to try it?'

'I'm always game to try something new.'

What about making love with me, with a choice of two beds?

She paused to get her breath back at the very thought.

'Me too,' he said.

'Before I go any further, we need to talk.' She looked up at him. It hurt to say this, as there was nothing she wanted more than to spend all the time with him. But she had to play the game. 'How do you see this trip going? I mean, do you want to do things together? Do you have an agenda? Or do we go our separate ways during the day? Maybe we meet up for dinner some nights?'

She had to be sure, one way or another, to make this work with Connor. They had the marriage certificate as proof they were legally married. But they needed to stay married—or at least appear to be married—until after that thirty-first of May deadline. Then, after an appropriate interval, Connor would become her ex-husband. Would their friendship be the same after spending so much time together?

Connor frowned. 'Why would we go our separate ways? I'd assumed we'd spend the time together. You'll want to meet with your family, I'm sure, and I'll need to spend some time online for Money Club business. But apart from that—'

'The family will want to meet you too. Remember, they think we're married. They'll want to meet my new husband. We'll have to play the role for them or it might get reported back to my grandparents.'

'I'd like to meet your cousins and any other members of your family. Your Australian family have been so good to me. It will be interesting to see what they're like here. Those who stayed.'

'I wasn't sure if you'd want to…to get that personal,' she said.

Connor put his hands on her shoulders and looked down into her face. 'Mock marriage aside, we're still friends, aren't we?'

'Of…of course we are.' She forced her voice to be steady. Cheerful, even.

Friends.

There it was again, that definitive word. It was as if he wanted to reiterate that friends was all they could ever be. In spite of those mixed messages he'd sent her at the wedding.

That kiss!

Or had she simply misread him? Was she deluding herself to think they could ever move outside the friend zone into something deeper. Even if it was simply friends with benefits?

'I can't imagine anyone who I'd rather see Budapest with than my best friend,' he said. 'Especially when I know how much this place means to you.'

'Me too,' she said. 'Be with you, I mean.' It was true. Should she really risk attempting to make it more than that?

They were married. That meant absolutely nothing—it was a means to an end. Connor had performed wonderfully in his role as bride-groom. She needed to forget anything other than he really was the best friend a person could ever have. And she couldn't risk losing that friendship.

Maybe her seduction plan wasn't such a great idea. She'd never seen a friends-with-benefits arrangement that had worked out. One partner always seemed to want more commitment and ended up getting hurt. Maybe it was the nature of intimacy that people got attached to people they had sex with. Not all the 'it doesn't mean anything' words in the world could change that. Did she want to risk that kind of pain? For her. Or, indeed, for Connor?

If Connor had invited her to Budapest on holiday a year ago, she would have jumped at the chance. She would treat the time here as if she and Connor were still just buddies. Separate-rooms-type buddies. That was all they'd been and all they were likely ever to be. She would enjoy this break in this beautiful city that had such significance to her family. But two weeks alone with Connor might be too much for her to hold off trying to seduce him, even staying in separate rooms. She wanted him so much. She might have to work out a way to go back to Australia earlier before she made a fool of herself.

'Budapest and my Hungarian heritage mean a lot to me,' she said.

'As they should.'

'I might have had an absent father, but I had grandparents who were determined to make up for Holt's absence. They're truly like second parents, as you well know. I grew up knowing I was Hungarian by descent. Our family here can be traced back a long time, through Hungary's turbulent history. Whereas I knew nothing much about my Waverly side—although my sisters have given me a crash course. I want to learn about what it means to be a Waverly of Garrison Downs without losing sight of how important my mother's family is to me too.'

'Of course you do,' he said. 'Remember when I said you must have inherited your love of horses from your father? I think your creative side comes from your Horvath family. That's such a part of you. You need to fully embrace it.'

Connor's kindness and understanding made her feel quite weepy. No one got her like he did. She sniffed. 'Sorry. Jet lag.'

'Come here.'

He pulled her into one of his special Connor bear hugs. She relaxed into it, resting her cheek against his shoulder as she had done so many times, feeling his strength surround her. She realised then that the nocturnal hand-holding had been the same kind of friendly comfort Connor's hugs had always been. There hadn't been any other meaning to it or anything sensual. She'd read too much into it.

'It's been quite the roller coaster for us over the last month or so,' he said. 'I wondered if we would get it all done on time. The trip to Garrison Downs. The engagement announcements. Then the wedding itself, with all that entailed. Mainly thanks to you, we pulled it off. You were brilliant. And worked so hard.'

'As the wedding was all about me, and what I would gain from it, me going all out to organise everything was to be expected. Fortunately, I'd resigned from my job to give me the time to act as wedding planner. It turned out to be a good party, though, didn't it?'

'The best of parties,' he said. 'I really enjoyed myself. In the end, I wasn't aware I was pretending. Like an actor who must get so deep into their role they say their lines without thinking.'

'Me too. I got so caught up in it. Accepting everyone's congratulations. Telling them how happy we were. Thanking them for the gifts they brought even though we stated no gifts. They'll have to be returned, of course.'

'And no one was any the wiser it wasn't real.'

'My mother had her doubts. But did you see how close she was to tears when she welcomed you as her son? Tears of joy, I mean. She ended up believing in us.'

Ana felt bad about that. Really bad. But she knew her mother would understand when she found out the truth. She wouldn't want her daughter's inheritance to be at risk because her daughter hadn't been able to find a real husband.

'Did anyone ask you if you were pregnant?' Connor said.

She laughed. 'My grandmother outright. Others skirted around it, but it was very obvious they thought it likely. A few of the older people actually stared at my stomach. Did anyone say anything to you?'

'Yes.'

She laughed. 'Some people simply don't have boundaries.'

'Did you tell Kartika the truth about the wedding?'

'I was nearly bursting with the need to talk to someone about what we were doing. Besides, she had to know. I asked her to be my bridesmaid at a fake wedding.'

'So, yes, then?'

'She can be trusted one hundred percent. She approved of our plan. I swear she would never tell anyone else. By the way, she said to say thank you, from one of my best friends to the other, for stepping up to help me.'

He paused. 'You were the most beautiful bride. I… I couldn't take my eyes off you.' His voice was husky and his arms tightened around her.

'Why thank you, dear friend,' she said, forcing her voice to sound light-hearted, glad her face was hidden from him. 'That means a lot, coming from you.'

'Seriously. You looked exquisite. Radiant. A dream bride to any man who—'

'Hadn't sworn off marriage?'

'Yes. Seeing you like that made me see you in a different way. As if a filter had overlaid a pre-existing image of my childhood friend. If… if things were different I—'

'You what, Connor?' she said, her heart racing. 'I would—'

The buzzer to their room sounded, shattering the moment.

Darn.

Most likely a bell boy, delivering their luggage. She decided to ignore it. But it buzzed again. It was too urgent to ignore. Regretfully, wishing she had just another minute—even a few seconds—to follow through on the conversation, she pulled away from Connor. Did she imagine he'd let her go with some reluctance? 'I'll get it,' she said. She opened the door.

'Your luggage, Mrs O'Neill,' the bell boy said.

Ana stilled. For a moment she was about to tell him he'd got the wrong room. No Mrs O'Neill here. But then she realised he meant *her.* She turned back to Connor. He was trying not to laugh at her disconcerted expression. 'That's you,' he said, his green eyes dancing.

'I… I guess it is,' she said.

For the time being, that is.

The bell boy wheeled the cart with their luggage to the larger of the two bedrooms. As anyone would, for a newlywed couple on their honeymoon. She thanked him, speaking in Hungarian, and tipped him with some Hungarian *forints.*

She turned back to Connor. The moment was lost. Would she ever know what he'd been about to say?

'Okay, Mr O'Neill, I guess we now have to toss for who gets the larger bedroom.'

'You, of course,' he said. 'I wouldn't be much of a gentleman if I nabbed it for myself.'

That was the trouble. She was hoping that, alone in this palatial suite, Connor might act less like a gentleman and more like a man who appreciated her as a desirable woman.

CHAPTER TEN

WHO WAS THIS WOMAN? Connor wondered. This
different Ana. Elegant, assured, *hot,* speaking
in rapid, confident Hungarian? She wasn't usually a person to draw attention to herself. A
hangover, he supposed, from having to keep
the truth about her father a secret. Yet here she
was in a short, tight black skirt, black tights,
cute little high-heeled boots he found incredibly sexy and an attention-getting red sweater
that hugged her curves. Perhaps it was because
no one in Budapest knew or cared about Holt
Waverly or his family. Ana could be just Ana.

And Connor liked it.

It was both exciting and perturbing to be in
such close quarters with this different version
of his long-time friend. He'd found it difficult
to keep that hug—what Ana always made a
thing of calling 'the Connor hug'—platonic and
comforting. When what he'd wanted to do was
pull her into his arms and kiss her. To take up

from where they'd started at the wedding. And not stop kissing her. Until kissing was no longer enough. What they should have continued at the airport hotel—if she hadn't fallen asleep.

He'd been saved by the buzzer from confessing that his feelings for her had changed. That since the wedding the idea of a bride—not just any bride, but an Ana bride—had seemed seductive rather than scary. He wanted her. And it was getting more difficult to hide it. He didn't want to push her into something she might not be ready for. It was difficult to tell if her feelings towards him had also evolved.

She was such a good actress. He didn't know any longer what was genuine and what was play-acting in aid of the mock marriage. That kiss at the wedding had seemed so real, so passionate, the kiss of a bride looking forward to her wedding night. But had it been part of the fake wedding game? A performance for the enjoyment of their guests? To have everyone there believing the marriage was the real deal? Had she not realised what she was doing by asking him to unlace her on their wedding night? Surely she couldn't be that naïve?

Back at Garrison Downs, before Christmas, she'd made such a fuss about the bed. He'd doubted she'd got any sleep on that poor excuse for a sofa, yet just now she'd seemed miffed that he'd booked her a room of her own. He didn't know any more exactly where he stood with her.

'I didn't know you could speak Hungarian,' he said.

'You mean after twenty years of friendship I can still surprise you?'

'Indeed you can,' he said. And he wasn't just referring to her language skills. 'I've heard you speak the odd words with your grandparents but you sounded so fluent talking to the bell boy.' The bell boy who had been discreetly ogling her. She looked so cute in that short, tight skirt. It taken him all he had to stop himself from telling the guy to keep his eyes off his wife.

'I told you I've been saving for a trip to Budapest. I decided that by the next visit I wanted to be able to speak the language. During the six months you were away in Sydney, I had some intensive lessons with Nagypapa. When he thought I was ready, he took me along to the Hungarian Club for conversation with his friends there. I'm pretty fluent now. The test will come when I get into conversations with people who won't make allowances for me.'

'You picked it up quickly,' he said admiringly. 'Well done.'

'Yes and no. I've always been surrounded by the language. Apparently, I had a lot of words when I was little. I learned Hungarian alongside English. Then I got to the stage I didn't want to stand out as different and refused to speak it any more.'

'But the language must have stayed in your subconscious.'

'I believe so. That's what my grandmother says. Anyway, it should make it easier for us to get around if I can speak the language. That said, English is widely spoken here. For example, the announcements on the metro are in both Hungarian and English. My cousins learned English at school.'

'I'm raring to get out there and see the city. To just walk around and get our bearings before we do any actual sightseeing.'

'Me too. We'll have to be careful what shoes we wear. A lot of where we'll be walking has cobblestones that might be slippery with the snow.'

'Understood,' he said.

'There's something else you need to know about Budapest.'

'And that is?'

'The food is amazing.'

He laughed. 'Like at your grandparents' restaurant? Then I'll love it.'

'There's traditional food to die for, but also contemporary food that borrows from other cuisines. While I was on the plane, I looked up some restaurants we might want to try. And I put together a list of sights we should see.'

'Won't you have seen it all before?'

'Not really. Remember, I was fifteen when I was first here and hanging out with family. Next time I was with a bunch of students just for one night. Now I'm with you.'

'And we're both so grown up and sophisticated.'

'Of course we are,' she said, striking a pose and pouting her mouth. Her lush, seductive mouth he'd kissed so thoroughly at the wedding. *Their* wedding.

When had she got so sexy?

The image of her with her wedding dress sliding off her shoulders as he unlaced her returned to taunt him.

'Shall we have quick showers and get going?' she said. She glanced down at her wrist. 'My watch has adjusted to Budapest time—that means lunch soon.'

'Lunch sounds good,' he said.

Surprisingly, he wasn't that hungry. He'd eaten so much on the plane. Then there was the fact his gut was twisted in knots about what he wanted to say to Ana. Would she welcome a change to the status quo? Did she want him the way he wanted her?

'We have his and her bathrooms,' she said. 'You go to yours and I'll go to mine.'

'Done,' he said, immediately revisiting the fantasy of being in the shower with her and helping her to soap her lovely, naked body.

'Oh, and, Connor?'

'Yes?'

'Don't shave.'

He put his hand to his bristly chin.

'I like that stubble,' she said, with a narrow-eyed, speculative look that made him wish he could tell what she was thinking. Because it seemed like it might be X-rated.

'Stubble stays,' he said, feeling bemused. And more than a touch aroused.

He was in and out of the shower as quickly as he usually was. But, surprisingly, he didn't have to wait overly long for Ana. He was in the short passageway between their rooms, still wrapped in the luxurious deep navy hotel robe, when she emerged from her bathroom wearing her robe. Disappointingly, it wrapped very tightly around her, giving no glimpse of curves.

Her face was set in a very determined expression, her cheeks flushed. 'You're here— good,' she said.

'What's up?' he asked. 'Something wrong with the shower? We can call housekeeping if there is.'

'There's absolutely nothing wrong with my shower. It's an excellent shower. No, it's me that's the problem.'

'You? Are you ill? You look okay but—'

She waved her hand dismissively. 'Nothing like that.'

'Then what?' he said, alarmed. He had never seen her like this.

'I have something to say to you and I'm not going to bottle it up any longer. I've been thinking about it in the shower.'

'Right,' he said. He wasn't sure what else he could say.

'I notice you didn't shave.'

'You asked me not to and I didn't.'

'Good,' she said. *'Argh!* There I go again. Prevaricating. Not saying what I really want to say. Although I really do like that stubble on you.'

'And what's that you want to say, Ana? Is it something I've done? Or not done? Let it rip.'

'It is and it isn't.' She started to wring her hands—not a good sign. He gently picked them up and disengaged her fingers. She scarcely seemed to notice.

'It's about me. Always feeling I need to think of others. Putting my own needs last. I think it dates back to the fact that my birth ruined my mother's life. And once I became aware of that I tried to make it up to her.'

'What? Your birth did no such thing. Your mother adores you.'

'I ruined her life,' she stated again. 'I wasn't really aware of it until I got older. Recently, I've thought about it a lot.'

'You really think that? I'll bet she doesn't. I know she thinks you're the best thing in life that ever happened to her. She actually told me that, just after we got engaged.'

'She was twenty-five with a promising career ahead of her. Then she was suddenly a single mother. Her chances of meeting someone else were immediately diminished. But she didn't want to date anyway. Not with a little girl to bring up. Then there was the complication of Holt. Always a presence in her life because of me. She would have preferred to put him firmly in her past.'

Connor noticed how Ana referred to her father by his given name, instead of Apa, when she was trying to look dispassionately at him.

'Mum was always concerned Holt would dump me as a daughter, the way he had dumped her. She constantly worried about money because she didn't trust him not to stop the allowance he paid her for my upkeep.'

He frowned. 'Do you think he would have stopped the allowance? That doesn't seem like something Holt would do.'

'How would we know? You talk a lot about trust. I don't think Mum ever trusted him again. By the time she actually fell for another man, it was too late for her to have a baby. I know she wanted more than one child. I had to make it up to her by…by being the best possible daughter.'

'You would have been that anyway. It's in your nature. I don't know why you can't see that.'

The same way he had difficulty coming to terms with his role in his parents' divorce? He hadn't known this was a scar from her past she bore. He'd been aware of some of it, but not the depth of what she was feeling now. Perhaps Ana being the same age as Lili had been when she'd met Holt had brought it front of her mind. He wanted to take her in his arms and hug her, tell her how wonderful she was. But it didn't seem the right moment.

'So I studied for a degree I didn't want to study,' she said. 'Got a job I don't like for the sake of security. To please not only my mother but also my grandparents. Now I'm doing it again.'

He frowned. 'What do you mean you're doing it again?'

'This holiday. This…this *honeymoon*. I asked you what you wanted to get out of it. Here. Budapest. But we didn't talk about what I wanted out of it. Maybe because you've paid for it and I don't want to be indebted to you.'

That stung. 'You could never be indebted to me.'

'I can pay you back once I inherit.' The flush on her cheeks was deepening.

He put his hands on her shoulders. The robe slipped to the side, baring her throat and the enticing curve of one breast.

'You will not pay me back. We don't work like that. We never have. Now, tell me what this is really about.' He spoke again before she had a chance to reply. 'I think I see where it's going. We didn't talk about what you expected from this holiday. That's me being male and selfish.'

Her eyes widened. 'No! No one could ever accuse you of being selfish. You're too perfect for that.'

His mouth twisted. 'Why does "perfect" said that way sound like an insult?'

'*Argh!* I'm getting it wrong again.' She looked up into his eyes, hers wide and sincere. 'I would never want to insult you. Ever. Or hurt you. You are, quite possibly, the most wonderful man alive.'

'I like that,' he said, taken aback.

'Good. You're meant to like it. And I mean every word.'

He felt he was still no closer to understanding what was bothering her. 'Ana, just tell me

what you want out of this holiday. If it's different from what I want, we can compromise.'
He liked to get straight to the point. But he'd learned over the years that Ana had her way of getting there. Usually in a circuitous manner that he had learned to navigate.

'Shower time is good for thinking,' she said. 'Negative ions from falling water inspire creativity.'

'I didn't know that,' he said, puzzled by her train of thought. Sometimes he really wondered if there was something in that 'men are from Mars and women from Venus' theory.

'I've always found it so. In fact, I came up with the idea for our best-selling earrings in the shower.'

'Okay...' he said.

'While I was in the shower just now, I decided I wasn't being honest with you about what I wanted. Because that's a difficult thing for me to do.'

He nodded, hoping it would encourage her to get to the point. He was distracted by the way her robe was falling off her shoulder. He doubted she wore anything at all underneath it.

'Okay,' she said. 'If I don't say this now, I probably won't ever say it.'

She took a deep breath. The robe slipped a

little further. Much more, and a nipple might come into sight.

'Understood,' he said.

'First, I am not Mrs O'Neill, so please don't call me that. Even if I was married for real, I would not be Mrs O'Neill. I don't mean that as an insult to you and your nice name. I wasn't deemed worthy of the Waverly name. Horvath will stay my name. It honours the people who wanted me and cared for me.'

'Okay,' he said. Curse Holt Waverly for leaving her with this legacy of insecurity. Despite everything Connor had said to her about claiming her rightful place in the Waverly family, that second-best feeling seemed to be lingering.

'Let's get another thing clear. I'm so over you thinking of me in a sisterly way.'

Funny, he'd had the same thought. He'd be glad to give up the role of protective older brother he'd played for so long. Now he had a different role in mind.

'Call me the girl next door, your horse-riding buddy, your friend…but *not* your sister.'

He felt deeply entrenched barriers falling away. Realised that he'd hidden behind the fiction that she was like a sister to him to stop himself from wanting her when circumstances hadn't been right for anything beyond friendship. Now there was nothing to stop him letting her know how he felt about her. The fake marriage had served to focus his thoughts on what a marriage might be between two people who had known each other most of their lives and who could truly trust each other.

She had more to say. 'I can assure you, I do not think of you that way. In fact, I fancy you like hell. I've been attracted to you since we were teenagers. I think you know that. And you've always let me down lightly when my attraction bubbles over and I throw myself at you. But if there is a reason for you to push me away—a real reason—then let me know. Just don't tell me it's because you think of me as a sister. There are better ways of telling me you're not attracted to me.'

He looked at her for a long, intense moment before he spoke. 'What makes you think I'm not attracted to you?'

Ana stared at Connor. He had never looked more handsome with his hair still damp from the shower, that sexy stubble, the dark robe loosely tied and open at his bare chest. He smelled deliciously of the designer toiletries from the bathroom that enhanced his natural, familiar Connor scent.

Her mouth suddenly went dry. 'Wh-what did you say?'

'Are you about to throw yourself at me again?'

'I'm… I'm considering it.' That was the whole point of her spiel.

'Then know this. I think you're beautiful, desirable and very, very sexy. I've spent years denying how attracted I am to you. Because you were too young. Because I needed things with you to stay the same when other parts of my life were spiralling out of control. Because I feared losing you if a relationship didn't work out. Because you had a boyfriend or I had a girlfriend, and the time wasn't right for us. No more denial. I've never wanted you more than I do at this moment.'

A delicious thrill tingled through her body at his words. The look in his green eyes told her even more.

'Are you serious?' she said.

'Very serious.'

'You're not teasing me? It would be cruel if you were teasing me, Connor.'

'I'm not teasing you, Ana. Are you teasing me about threatening to throw yourself at me?'

'Of course not. I mean, I'm not teasing you. Or threatening you. I want you too.' Her voice broke. 'So much.' This was Connor offering everything she wanted from him.

His eyes narrowed in a very sensuous way she had never seen before in their twenty years of friendship. It sent shivers of awareness coursing through her. She felt his gaze on where her robe was slipping off her bare shoulder.

'How do you plan to go about throwing yourself at me?' he said, his voice deep and throaty.

'Um…' She was so surprised and pleased at his response, she hadn't actually planned the logistics of a seduction. The staged unlacing of her wedding gown hadn't done the trick.

'Do you plan to take a run at me and fling yourself against my chest?'

She laughed at the image that conjured up. 'No. Don't be silly.'

'How, then? Would you care to demonstrate?'

She smiled, a slow smile of appreciation of this gorgeous, gorgeous man she wanted so much. Had wanted for so long. And who she knew so well. But as a friend, not a lover. She stepped closer and looked up at him, her gaze intent on his face. Her heart started to race at the awareness in his eyes, the sensual set of his mouth.

This was Connor, but not a Connor she had seen before. A private Connor for her eyes only. She wanted to know him as a lover. She wound her arms around his neck, drew his head down to hers and kissed him.

It wasn't a show kiss for the benefit of anyone watching. Or a practice kiss. It was a kiss that came from her heart, singing a message to him that she was his to take. Kissing Connor. Wanting Connor. His tongue slid between her lips to meet hers, and the kiss quickly moved from tentative to exciting, to passionate and demanding. All those years had passed since their last proper kiss. It was just as exhilarating, just as arousing, just plain wonderful. She wanted so much more than kisses. But she would enjoy these kisses in the meantime.

She broke away to steady herself, to catch her breath, to make sure this was real.

'Why haven't we done this before?' she said, her heart beating in triple time, her breath ragged.

'Because we weren't ready,' he said simply.

Through her haze of excitement and mounting desire, she realised he was right. This was the right time for them. Whatever came of this, she would have no regrets. They had time, opportunity, privacy and a choice of two beds.

'Is this what you want?' he said. 'Because if you'd rather wait—'

'Wait for what, Connor?' she said, teasing.

'For us to make love,' he said, his voice husky.

She was ready. Oh, yes, she was. She was very aware he was naked under his robe. And it was obvious he was ready to take this sensual adventure further.

'I'm ready when you are,' she said. Then

laughed. A bit too nervously. A bit too giggly. 'That's something I would have said to you when we were teenagers. Sorry.'

'No need to apologise. I think it's cute. And I take that for consent.'

'It's consent, all right,' she said. A rush of desire for him made her feel suddenly light-headed, her nipples pebbling and aching for his touch.

He pushed the robe off her shoulders so it slid away from her breasts to rumple at her waist. She was baring her breasts to Connor. And it felt so right.

'You're beautiful,' he said huskily, cupping her breasts in his strong, sure hands, caressing her nipples until pleasure shot through every pleasure pathway, heading straight to between her legs. 'Absolutely beautiful.'

'I… I'm glad you think so,' she murmured. 'You're pretty darn beautiful yourself.'

With hands that trembled with impatience, she pushed his robe away to plant her hands on his hard, warm chest. She was met with an impressive wall of muscle; he really had been working out. She kissed from the smooth hollow beneath his ears, along his chin, knowing her face would be red from the pleasing scrape of his stubble, but not caring as it felt so good, until she met his mouth to claim it again in a kiss.

He kissed her back, hungry and possessive. Then broke away to plant small warm, kisses down her neck until he reached her breasts. She gasped her pleasure and delight, moaned when he kissed and tongued one nipple while rolling the other between his fingers.

She realised she had pushed him up against the wall, too overcome by passion to really be aware of what she was doing. Until he broke away from the kiss.

'Shall we take this somewhere more comfortable?' he said, panting.

'Good idea,' she said, holding on to him for support.

'Your bed or mine?'

'Whichever is closest. The carpet will do at a pinch.'

He looked a little shocked 'You continue to surprise me.'

'I hope I never stop surprising you,' she said with a teasing smile.

'I look forward to lots of surprises.' He swung her up in his arms.

'Connor! This is so romantic. But you don't have to carry me.'

'But I want to. Besides, you're very light.'

'You're very strong.'

He made carrying her seem effortless. He took her to the nearest bed, which happened to be his, and laid her down on it. He undid the ties from her robe, she did the same for him and they were both completely naked. Her hungry gaze took in his perfect male body. Broad shoulders, powerful chest, six pack, long, strong limbs. She had to clear her throat before she spoke.

'It's a long time since I've seen you without clothes. You've changed.'

He laughed. 'I should hope so. That was a long time ago. I was most likely running around under the garden hose with my brother.'

'We were so innocent. There must have come a time when our parents decided we were too old for naked shenanigans and sharing a room but I don't remember.'

She walked her fingers down across his chest, admiring, wanting. 'I should be feeling awkward, being naked. I don't think you've even seen me in a bikini since I got my first training bra.'

'You've got absolutely nothing to feel awkward about,' he said. 'You've got a lovely body. The loveliest.'

The transition from just friends to something altogether more intimate seemed so relaxed, easy and incredibly exciting.

'This is different, isn't it?' she said breathlessly. 'Crossing boundaries into the unexplored.

We're so familiar with each other and yet this is so very different.'

'Can you stop analysing this and just enjoy it?' His voice was hoarse.

'Yes, I— *Oh!*'

She couldn't have spoken more even if she'd wanted to. All she could think about was the intense pleasure of Connor caressing her in her most intimate places. He seemed to know intuitively what would please and arouse her. She bucked against his hand, aching for more. Wanting him inside her. But not completely oblivious.

'Protection?' she managed to choke out.

'Got it.' He reached to the nightstand beside the bed. Connor donning a condom was a sight she had never imagined she would see. She found it incredibly arousing. She offered to help. He offered no objection.

'Now,' she said. 'I need you. Please.'

When Connor pushed inside her, she felt utterly complete. They found each other's rhythms straight away, each stroke sheer ecstasy, building to the peak. She came with a cry of intense ecstasy, followed by Connor's shout of release.

For a moment she lay close to him, still shaken by the power of her orgasm, the intensity of her joy in having him so close.

'Yeah. I know,' he said.

'What do you mean, *you know*? I didn't say anything.'

'You were going to say, why did we wait so long, weren't you?'

'How did you know I was going to say that?'

'I know you so well.'

At the same time, she answered her own question. 'Because we know each other so well.' Making love with Connor was everything she'd fantasised it to be and more. There was a connection that was way more than physical. She laughed and Connor did too. Then they started to make love all over again, completely in tune with each other's needs.

Much later, she lay replete within the circle of her best friend's arms.

Best friend to best lover.

'Connor?' she murmured sleepily.

'Yes?'

'That was better than the very best Connor hug.'

'I should hope so,' he said, smiling. It was the indulgent smile he gave her when she said something he found particularly cute.

'Like a hug with benefits.'

'A hug on steroids.'

Now completely unselfconscious about her nudity, she lifted herself up on her elbow so she could see his face. 'You know this changes everything?'

'I know.'

'We won't be able to go back to being just friends.'

'Who would want to?' he said. 'Friends is good. Lovers is better.'

'Agreed,' she murmured. Best friends and lovers—what more could she want?

CHAPTER ELEVEN

FOUR DAYS LATER, Ana found herself in jeweller's heaven—her great-uncle Istvan's jewellery store in downtown Pest. She loved the traditional opulence of it all. Plush carpet. Chandeliers. Display cabinets of mellow timbers and spotless glass that showcased necklaces, bracelets, rings and earrings made from glittering diamonds and precious coloured gems such as sapphires, emeralds and rubies, as well as semi-precious gems. There were both classic and contemporary styles. Small breakout rooms were as much for security as the comfort and privacy of clients trying on fine jewellery with an attentive salesperson. She could have spent hours browsing and admiring the exquisite creations, all made here.

But what interested her most was the design studio and workshop on the floor above. When she'd been fifteen, it had been like stepping into another world, one where she'd immediately known she belonged.

Her uncle—so like his brother, her beloved grandfather Zoltan—took her upstairs. At the entrance to the studio, she stood in awe. There was an artisan seated at each work station, concentrating on the intricate task of hand-crafting fine jewellery. She breathed in the subtle scent of solder and melting wax.

'I'm seeing this room through different eyes,' she said. 'When I was fifteen, I knew nothing about jewellery making. Now I truly appreciate what I'm seeing here. Yet, in some ways it seems different. Not surprising, as it's ten years later.'

'Traditional techniques are at the very heart of our craft. However, we also keep up to date with new technology. Lasers, computer-driven programs and 3D wax printers are something I would never have dreamed of when I was your age. Yet they have earned their place here along with our more traditional tools.'

Ana looked around her with even more respect. 'I'm so looking forward to spending the morning here with you. There's so much I know I still need to learn.'

'It's a shame you can't spend more time with us. I know you've studied in Australia, but there's nothing like working in a studio like this to really hone your skills. Only one of my grandchildren has followed me into the business. I like that my Australian great-niece also shares the interest. Your online store is inspiring. I know this is your honeymoon, but maybe you could consider returning to Budapest to spend more time here. Perhaps for six months?'

'Seriously? You'd have me here? Working? Learning?'

'The door is always open for you and your charming new husband. You both could stay with your great-aunt and me.'

'That's a wonderful invitation. I would love it. Six months might be too much time away from home. But three months? Perhaps later in the year?'

'Whatever is convenient for you.'

Ana was dreading the time when she and Connor would end their marriage of convenience and file for divorce. No matter which way they explained it, their families would feel at best upset, at worst deceived. And she would be heartbroken. Because it would be the end of her friendship with him. How could she possibly return to just friends after all they'd shared on this honeymoon? How could she bear to hear him talk about his latest girlfriend? Or make plans for his life that didn't include her? Three months in Budapest away from him, away from everything at home, would be a good escape.

The next day, Connor sat holding hands with Ana on a sight-seeing cruise boat. It was taking them on an hour-long round trip to see some of the Budapest sights from the vantage point of the River Danube. She was bundled up in a quilted puffer coat, wearing boots, a hat and gloves. So was he. It was the fifth day of their honeymoon and they had managed to see up close and inside several of the fabulous neo-Gothic buildings they now viewed from the river from a different perspective. After they'd managed to drag themselves out of the bed-room, that was. But wasn't that what honey-mooners did? Made love at any opportunity?

The boat passed the magnificent Houses of Parliament, so expansive they seemed to take up most of the river frontage on the Pest side. They had been one of the first of the beautiful Budapest buildings they'd visited. The next day, they'd walked over the Chain Bridge and taken the steep funicular up Castle Hill to explore the castle and the Fisherman's Bastion, with its multitude of turrets. They'd listened to a clas-sical music concert in the ornately beautiful Matthias Church. Then walked around the well-preserved old town, marvelling at how lovely it was. On another day, they'd listened to a choir in the awe-inspiring St Stephen's Basilica back on the Pest side.

But what Connor had enjoyed most was wandering around downtown Pest with Ana, just taking in the Opera House, the galleries, shops, cafes, restaurants and the various landmarks. He was fascinated by a different city and a different way of life. When they'd veered off the main streets, they'd found themselves in a cobbled square around an ornate fountain, as if they'd stepped back in time. Or they'd come across a monument to a long-ago prince or general on horseback. There seemed to be a lot of equestrian monuments in Budapest, much to Ana's and his delight. They'd taken selfies in front of each one they'd encountered.

Ana had exclaimed at the number of posters promoting art galleries, concerts, the ballet and the opera—Budapest was a cultural city. The previous day, she'd spent a morning with her Great-Uncle Istvan in his jeweller's workshop, learning from him. Connor had roamed the city on his own. 'More of a case of learning how much I didn't know about designing and making jewellery,' she'd told him on her return.

The previous night Ana's second cousins— the children of her mother's cousins, who were around the same age as Ana—took them on a ruin bar crawl, which had been a lot of fun. The cousins had been amazed at Ana's fluent Hungarian.

Yesterday afternoon they'd braved one of the thermal mineral spas for which Budapest was famed. They'd chosen the elegant art nouveau Gellert private baths in Buda for their experience. Connor hadn't really cared much for sitting in his swimming trunks in a large bath of very hot mineralised water, full of strangers, then getting into another even hotter one. But Ana had loved the experience, telling him it was very good for the skin. She wanted to go back.

Another welcome discovery about Budapest was that the food was every bit as good as Ana had assured him it would be. They'd eaten in a traditional Hungarian restaurant, serenaded by violinists playing folk music, and had been offered Tokaji, the famous Hungarian sweet dessert wine. Another memorable meal had been in the downtown Market Hall, which they had discovered by chance as they'd walked around the area. Duck breast and red cabbage served in enamel bowls in a fashionable restaurant overlooking the river to Buda had been another highlight.

A disproportionate number of meals had been delivered to Ana and him via room service as they'd made up for lost time in bed. He was greedier for Ana than he was for food. And she seemed to feel the same way about him.

Ana's wise grandfather, Zoltan, had told him Ana needed to spend time in Budapest. To appreciate that her heritage was as much this cultured and sophisticated city as it was the Outback of South Australia. To appreciate that she didn't need to feel second best because of the way her father had deprived her of knowledge of her Australian family. What pleased Connor most of all about this trip was that it was having exactly the effect he'd hoped on Ana. He had never seen her happier or more confident in herself as a person.

He watched her now. They were each listening to a headphone commentary of the landmarks along the river. His was in English. Ana had chosen to have the Hungarian one, as she wanted to expose herself to as much of the language she could while they were in Budapest. The descriptions of the landmarks were interspersed with the music of Franz Liszt, Hungary's famous nineteenth-century composer.

The trouble with them being on holiday in such a different place, discovering a whole new relationship as lovers, was that talk of the future had been put on hold. During these honeymoon days—and nights—discovering each other in a very different way, he'd decided he wanted to secure a future with Ana. Forget this pretend marriage scenario. He wanted her as his wife for real. He just hoped she felt the same.

There were just a few plans to fall into place before he actually said anything to her. The most important of those plans was buying a house. Not just any house, but a house in St Kilda that Ana had always liked. It was a grand old house in the style Australians termed 'Federation'. They'd passed the house when walking home from primary school. Even then she'd liked it.

After they'd announced their 'engagement', he and Ana had discussed where they would live after the wedding. They'd decided on her house, which made sense. She had a guest bedroom and she didn't care for his ultra-modern apartment. Truth be told, neither did he. It was more an investment than a home. All his real estate purchases had been investments. Back in Melbourne, Ana had told him that, once her inheritance was settled, she intended to knock on the door of the house she admired and make an offer for it. Ana knew from chatting over the fence with the widowed owner that the large house and garden were getting too much for her.

The day after they'd first made love, Connor

had instructed an estate agent to negotiate the purchase of the house on his behalf. It would be an excellent house for them to live and later raise a family in. That was how serious he was about making this mock marriage a real one. He loved her and he wanted her as his wife. But how did he talk marriage to a woman to whom he was already married, and who had repeatedly said didn't want to be tied down by marriage?

It was snowing in Budapest, big, white flakes drifting slowly down from the sky to frost with white everywhere it landed. But it was as if the sun was shining in Ana's heart. Exploring the city with Connor was like carrying her own sunshine with her. After the river tour ended, they strolled hand in hand from the dock back towards their hotel. She couldn't bear to let go of his hand. Had to keep glancing up to reassure herself he was there. When he caught her eye, his smile reassured her. Then he dropped a kiss on her mouth, their lips frosty cold.

So this was what it was like to be in love—truly in love. She loved Connor. She couldn't deny it for a second longer. She'd never felt anything for anyone else that came close to her feelings for him. Something about him called to her heart like no one else had.

She'd fallen in love with him back when she'd been fifteen, about the time of that first kiss. She hadn't been too young to fall in love—maybe too young to do anything about it, but not too young to feel that emotion as fiercely as she had. She'd never fallen out of love with him. Just repressed it and denied it. No wonder she'd never found love with anyone else. Her heart had put the shutters up against anyone who wasn't Connor.

Did he feel the same for her? Sometimes she thought so. Other times she couldn't be sure. They'd certainly crossed out of the friend zone. The sex was amazing—passionate, energetic, tender at times. But, emotionally, she wasn't sure if Connor felt the same way she did. There was the friendly banter, laughs and multiple orgasms. But was there love? And, even if there was love, was there a future?

As far as the mock marriage went, they were still in the same uncertain place. Connor hadn't changed his views on trust and commitment. Or, if he had, he certainly hadn't told her. Was this a friends-with-benefits scenario? She'd never been in such an arrangement to know. Was the plan to stay lovers once the honeymoon was over and they were back to faking a marriage in Melbourne? They had discussed, to keep up the pretence, he would move into her house for as long as it took for the inheritance to come through. Then they'd separate and divorce proceedings would commence once the statutory year of separation had passed. One way or the other, that wouldn't be later than the end of May. Rose would either marry or she wouldn't by that date.

The uncertainty was beginning to make Ana feel edgy again. She would have to say something to Connor. But that wouldn't be easy. She didn't know how or where to start. She thought about it with every step on the walk back to the hotel.

When they got back to their suite, they took off their warm coats and boots. But not for long. Almost straight away, Connor got a call which he took in the other room. 'I'm going to have to go out again,' he said, when he came back.

Darn. Further delay in that much-needed talk about their future.

'Money Club business?'

'No.'

'Shopping?'

'No.'

'Don't tell me—you're sneaking out for another thermal bath?'

'No.' He seemed distracted, as if he'd barely heard her. He hadn't even cracked a smile at the thought of him visiting the spa. 'I'll tell you when we catch up again. Can we meet at that coffee house in an hour? I know you love it and want to go there again.'

Ana's grandmother had taken her to the splendidly ornate coffee house on Vörösmarty Square on her first visit to Budapest when she'd been fifteen. It was a combined café, cake shop and chocolate shop. What wasn't there to love about it?

But her mouth went dry at Connor's evasiveness. Why would he want to go out in Budapest without her? Was he already tiring of her non-stop company? After all, it wasn't a real honeymoon.

Her old insecurities came rushing back. *Was it something she'd done wrong?* Suddenly she didn't feel at all like coffee and a slice of *dobos torte*.

'Sure. I'll see you there in an hour,' she said, forcing her voice to sound normal.

He'd been gone for half an hour when his phone rang. In his rush to go out, he'd left it on the table in the living area. She let it ring out, but it rang again. There was something about an insistently ringing phone that got to her. She picked it up.

'Connor O'Neill's phone,' she said.

'May I speak to Connor, please?' It was a man's voice.

'I'm afraid he's not here; can I take a message for you?'

'Is that Mrs O'Neill?' Again, her mind went momentarily blank at the name.

'Yes. Yes, it is.'

The man identified himself as a St Kilda estate agent. 'Could you please tell him, the sale completed half an hour ago. He's now the owner of a magnificent house in St Kilda.'

The agent told her the address. She knew the house only too well. A big, old, turn-of-the-twentieth-century house on one of the best streets in St Kilda. She used to walk past it on the way to the restaurant from school. All gabled roofs, ornate carved wood trims and stained glass. A beautiful house she had seen deteriorate in recent years as the upkeep had become too much for the elderly widow who lived there. Worth multiple millions. It was her dream house. She'd planned to buy it when her inheritance came through. Why would Connor buy it for himself when he knew how much she wanted it? Knowing him, it wouldn't even be to live in. It would be as an investment.

'Congratulations, Mrs O'Neill,' the agent said.

'Th…thank you,' she said, and disconnected the call.

Connor had bought a house? That house?

And he hadn't told her. Why? There was no real reason he should tell her of his business dealings. But a house. A house was such a personal thing. That particular house was so beautiful. It should be *her* house, not an investment for the Money Club.

She slipped on her coat and gloves. She wasn't wearing the lavish engagement ring. She'd taken it off when she'd spent time with her great-uncle and hadn't put it back on. He would spot it as a lab-made diamond and might ask questions. Not that there was anything wrong with lab-made. Some found that kind of diamond more ethical and environmentally friendly. But a lab-made diamond lacked the tiny imperfections of one that had formed underground over millions of years. Fake. Like her marriage to Connor.

Her feet dragged as she made her way over the slippery, cobbled streets to the coffee shop. For the first time, she felt reluctant to see her friend. She would have to challenge him about the house and she didn't like confrontations. She loved that house. He would probably maximise profit by turning it into apartments or, worse, pull it down and rebuild.

He was there at a table, waiting for her. She could tell by the tense set of his shoulders something had happened. She hung her coat on a rack and went towards him. He got up to greet her, unsmiling. Why? What had happened after he'd left the hotel? What had the call been about that had taken him away from her? And what had upset him? It couldn't be as bad as picking up the phone to find her fake husband had gazumped her on the house she'd told him she intended to buy. He was a fine person to talk about trust.

She certainly didn't feel like smiling. In fact, she could hardly bear to look at him. They exchanged terse greetings. She didn't meet his gaze. The waiter took her order for coffee. No cake; it would choke her. She took out his phone from her shoulder bag and slid it across the table to him.

'Thank you,' he said, taking it. 'I realised I'd left it behind when it was too late to turn back.'

'I answered a call for you,' she said.

He frowned. 'Who from?'

'An estate agent in Melbourne. It's very late in the day there. Congratulations. Apparently you're the owner of a beautiful Federation house in St Kilda. The sale just completed.'

'Good,' he said, still unsmiling. 'I was waiting for that news.'

'Why did you keep that secret from me, Connor—that you'd gazumped me on the house I told you I wanted to buy? I know we're not really husband and wife, but we are friends.' *Just friends.* 'You didn't need to exclude me.'

'I wanted to wait until the sale actually completed. And tell you when we had a talk about our future.'

'And when was that going to be?' she said.

He leaned across the table towards her. 'Perhaps after you told me you were planning to spend three months living in Budapest and working with your great-uncle.'

She gasped. 'How did you—?'

'Find out about that?'

'Yes.'

'That call I took back in the hotel was from your great-uncle.'

'Why would he call you?'

'He thinks I'm your husband, for one thing. Is it true? Are you planning to come and live here? I can't believe you didn't tell me.' Connor's mouth was set in a tight line, his eyes cold.

'It was something I discussed with him, yes. An idea—more his idea than mine, actually. I could learn so much from him. But, Connor, I wouldn't do that without talking it over with you.'

'Wouldn't you?' he said.

'Like I wouldn't buy a house without telling you. Especially if I knew it was your dream house. Especially after the last few days. I thought… I thought we'd… Never mind.'

'I wanted it to be a surprise for you.'

'For me? Really? Why would you make a purchase like that without involving me? I'm really over people making decisions on my behalf. My parents. My grandparents. Surely not you too?'

He frowned. 'It seemed the right thing to do. I knew you'd always liked that house. I'd planned to buy in St Kilda for a while. I had estate agents keeping an eye out for the right house for me from back when I was living in Sydney. The agent told me only recently that particular house had just gone up for sale. There was immediate interest in it. I had to move quickly to secure it.'

'It actually went on the market? What happened to the old lady who lived there?'

'She's gone to live with her daughter. It got too much for her to upkeep.'

So she would have missed out on the house anyway. The owner had told her she would contact her if she was thinking of selling, but the lovely lady's memory probably wasn't the best. Still, it was a decision she should have made for herself.

'I'm glad. For her, I mean. She was a nice old lady. I'm glad she's being looked after.'

'Her family knew the value of the place right down to the last cent.'

'Lucky you got it, then,' she said. She still couldn't understand why he hadn't told her.

'Not luck. Hard negotiating skills,' he said. 'Seriously. I bought the house for you, Ana. Because I knew how much you loved it. Not to control you, but for us to make a home together. I really wanted to surprise you. A wedding present, if you will. But, if you feel so strongly about it, how about I put the house in your name? Then, when you inherit, you can buy me out.'

Make a home together? What did he mean by that? 'You'd do that? You'd seriously do that?' she said.

'Yes,' he said. 'If it makes you less cranky with me. I could see us living there.'

'As…as friends?'

'We'll always be friends.'

Her heart sank. *Just friends.*

His gaze was intent, searching. 'But also as more than friends. As…as a couple.'

'Seriously?' Ana paused to take in the import of what he'd said.

He nodded. 'But then I heard you're planning to live in Budapest. Without saying a word to me.'

'You know why I talked to my great-uncle

about coming here to live?' She kept her voice low. The café was large and busy, but she didn't want such a private conversation to be over-heard. 'It was because when we got divorced, as planned, I would have somewhere to run to. My escape. I would have to be far away. It would be too painful to have to see you. My ex-husband.'

Connor frowned. 'When Great-Uncle Istvan told me about the visit, I assumed you wanted to get out of the mock to come and live here. To put me behind you.'

'That's not what I want at all,' she said, her voice unsteady.

'Me neither,' he said.

'I love you, Connor.' The 'L' word slipped out without her planning it. 'There. I've said it.' *She felt it.* 'The thought of not being with you is unbearable. You talk about being a couple, yet we've said nothing about a future with each other. And…and we're in the situation where we're married but not really married.'

The Connor smile was back, easing the tense lines of his face. 'You love me? As more than a friend?'

'Yes,' she said. 'I think I've always loved you. There I go, throwing myself at you again.'

He reached over the table to take both her hands in his. His green eyes searched her face.

'I love you too, Ana. With all my heart. I believe I've always loved you. I just didn't recognise it.'

'Can you say that again, please? The "I love you", I mean? I really, really like the sound of it.' She was smiling, at the same time trying to stave off tears of joy.

'I'll say it as many times as you want. These last few days have been the happiest of my life.'

'Oh, Connor.' She blinked to hold back the tears. 'I… I can't tell you how happy that makes me. I love you so much.'

'If that's what you want, I'll say I love you twenty times a day for a lifetime,' he said. 'I want us to stay married. To have a real marriage. A committed marriage.'

'But…but you said you didn't want to get married. For real, I mean. You didn't trust yourself to not act like your father.'

'And you said you wanted to fly free without being tied down by marriage.'

'Marriage to anyone but you, I meant,' she said. 'I know you won't clip my wings, Connor.'

'When it comes to loving you, I trust you. More importantly, I trust myself,' he said.

She kissed him across the table. 'I've always known I could trust you.'

'I know you have. You've always believed in me.'

'And you've always been on my side.'

'I want us to live in that house together, Ana. I bought it for us. It needs total renovation, but I think you would enjoy that. It's a family home. We could raise a family there.'

'A family? We're talking children?'

'Yes. A real marriage. With everything that comes with it: Children. A dog. A cat. When we're both ready, that is. I don't want to push you into anything.'

'I couldn't think of anything more wonderful,' she said, kissing him again. It was a sweet kiss of affirmation, love and a happiness that was bubbling through her.

Connor pulled back from the kiss. 'You haven't asked me why your great-uncle called me. It's unlike you not to be more curious.'

'I've been too busy being happy that you love me like I love you. But now I'm curious. Why did he call you?'

Connor pulled a small velvet box from his jacket pocket. It had her uncle's store logo engraved on it. 'He called me to tell me this was ready to pick up.'

'You bought me jewellery?'

Connor flipped open the box and took out a ring. A gorgeous blue sapphire, baguette-cut, flanked by two baguette diamonds on a fine platinum band.

Ana gasped. 'Connor, that's my dream ring.'

'I know. I remember you telling me that's what you'd make for yourself. I thought, if we're going to have a real marriage, we should have a real engagement ring.'

She kissed him again. 'It's perfect. Absolutely perfect. And made by my great-uncle, which makes it even more perfect. What did you tell him?'

'That you didn't much care for the diamond ring I'd chosen for you. That I wanted to get you a ring that you'd love, as you'd be wearing it for the rest of your life.'

'He'd understand that.'

'So how do I propose to a woman I'm already married to?' Connor paused for a breath. 'Ana, my love, will you be my wife—my wife for real?'

Ana thought her heart would burst with happiness. 'Oh, yes, Connor. Yes, yes and yes!'

He slid the ring over her wedding band on the third finger of her left hand and kissed her again. 'I love you.'

'I love you too.' She would never tire of saying it.

There was a smattering of polite applause. Ana looked around to see they had quite an audience of smiling people at the tables nearby. She held up her hand to show them her ring and smiled, her heart so full of joy she wanted to share it with the world.

She was Connor's wife. And she'd found the best of all possible husbands living next door.

EPILOGUE

*Garrison Downs,
first week of February, summer*

GARRISON DOWNS IN February was sweltering. The sun beat down from a sky bluer than the bluest Waverly eyes onto the red dirt and thirsty grey foliage. It was too hot even for insects to hum. From the homestead gardens wafted the light, fresh scent of lavender. Could there be a greater contrast to the snow-frosted Budapest she and Connor had left just ten days ago, Ana thought.

And this time Ana had a feeling of coming home. That she belonged here on the sprawling Outback kingdom of the Waverlys. Not a permanent home. Not that. Not now. Maybe not ever. Her life with Connor was in Melbourne. And Budapest too.

They had already started work on the restoration of the St Kilda mansion which they planned to make their permanent home. The major work would be done while they spent three months in Budapest—she working with her great-uncle, Connor working with an international veterinary aid organisation. Their house would be ready for them when they got back. Connor joked that he hoped there would be nice neighbours, so that any children they might be blessed with could make friends with the kids next door. After all, that was how he'd met his wife when she had come hurtling through the hedge.

But that was for the future. The reason Ana felt at home here now was not so much the property, the cattle business, the beautiful homestead or even the horses. What would keep her coming back to Garrison Downs was her sisters. That was why she was here now, for the unveiling of the new portrait of all four of them.

Rose, Eve and Tilly had brought unimagined joy into her life—they were the greatest gifts her father had bequeathed to her. The Horvath family had also embraced the sisters as new family members brought into the fold. It turned out Lili had spent quite some time with Rose and Eve at the wedding. Past resentments and pain had been well and truly buried. Eve's baby, due in June, would be welcomed with excitement and love as the first grandchild in the extended family.

Ana's friendship circle had also been widened by the men her sisters had married. On their recent visit to Chaleur, she and Connor had immediately connected with the charming Prince Henri, who made Princess Matilda so happy. Nate had become a friend too, as well as their trusted lawyer.

There was just the one dim cloud on the horizon of her bright future at Garrison Downs. All four sisters had to be married by the end of May. Three of them were now married. Only Rose remained unwed. Her oldest sister had assured the others not to worry, there were plans afoot. But she would give no further detail. It wasn't in Rose's nature to tantalise, but tantalise she had with that hint that her husband hunt had commenced. It remained for them all to see how it ended. Ana felt confident that Rose would never allow Garrison Downs to fall out of Waverly hands.

Another reason that Ana now felt at home here, was that the ongoing speculation and gossip swirling around the family since her father's death had been addressed by a public acknowledgement of her. The Waverly family had just released a carefully worded statement to the press. It welcomed into the family Holt's youngest daughter to a woman other than his wife, their half-sister, Anastasia. The statement had finally lifted the oppressive shadow of se-

crecy she had lived under all her life. Already
there was avid interest in such a juicy story. All
media requests for interviews and background
material were being professionally handled by
Eve, the family's own PR maven. Eve would
fiercely protect their privacy and dignity.

The unveiling of the new portrait of the four
Waverly sisters had now become symbolic of
their unity. Eve had suggested the painting
might even become a focus for a carefully cu-
rated story about the newly united family to
feature in one of the weekend newspaper mag-
azines. The large painting was to be hung in
the family dining room in the space vacated by
the old one. The sisters had commissioned the
same eminent artist who had painted the original portrait, as well as the portrait of Holt that
hung in his study. He'd been a friend of Holt.
It was in honour of Holt's memory that he had
come out of retirement to do the new portrait.
In return for a hefty fee, of course.

With Tilly in Chaleur, the four sisters weren't
able to come together at the same time to pose
for the portrait. On her previous visit, Ana had
followed the artist's instructions to pose infor-
mally with Rose and Eve on the steps of the
back veranda of the homestead, near the big,
old dented metal bell that was a feature. Lindy,
the housekeeper, had stood in for Tilly, even

though she was a head shorter. The artist had then painted from photographs and his memories of Garrison Downs, which he had visited on many occasions.

The bell used to be attached to the original old settler's cottage to call back home for meals the workers of generations gone by. As children, the three older sisters had known it as a signal to cease whatever mischief they were up to outside and come in.

Now the sisters and the two husbands headed into the cool of the air-conditioned homestead to view the portrait. Ana couldn't help a gasp when she saw it, echoed by both of her nearby sisters and Tilly, watching via video. Connor held her hand in a firm grip. Her beloved husband knew this would be an emotional moment for her. He was there, as he always had been, caring for her and supporting her. They'd gone from friends to lovers. Lovers was infinitely better!

The portrait, done in oils and entitled *Sisters*, was outstanding, breath-taking in the way it portrayed its subjects. Not only did it capture the beauty of the four young women but somehow also their intelligence, kindness and the pleasure they took in each other's company. The significance of the bell was that it had called the four sisters home and would continue to call them home at different times of their lives.

Although their colourings were different, there was a facial resemblance in all four of the sisters that clearly showed they were related. But it was the Waverly eyes, masterfully painted to look so blue and alive, that were the ultimate proof of their shared DNA.

Eve had suggested they all wear blue. It had been a genius idea. Rose wore a tailored trouser suit in a deep powder-blue, brown hair pulled back in her signature ponytail. She, the boss, was closest to the bell.

Tilly was carefree in denim overalls, with her luxuriant blonde hair flowing loose below her shoulders and her wide, generous smile caught halfway to laughter. She sat on the top step, her knees hugged to her chest.

Eve looked elegant in a fitted pencil dress in a clear ice-blue that didn't show her baby bump at all. Her pale-blonde hair was pulled back in a bun, her expression relaxed and open to all the happiness that had found her.

Ana was pleased with the way she was portrayed—close, connected, very much a part of it, as if she had always been on that veranda with her sisters. She wore a pretty dress with big puffed sleeves in the softest shade of indigo.

Her black hair was in a messy bun, soft tendrils framing her face and gentle, thoughtful smile.

Integral to the portrait were the sister bracelets Ana had crafted for each of them with intuition and affection. Also connecting all four sisters was River. The big old border collie, his head resting on his front paws, lay by Rose's feet, the other three sisters within patting distance. The artist had captured River's sweet doggy smile and caught his long, feathery tail mid-thump.

'I think we all scrub up well,' said Rose, pride in her family underscoring her voice.

'Yes, we do,' said Eve. 'I can't fault a thing.'

'I just wish I could be there to hug you all,' said Tilly, through the video phone, her voice shaky. Her royal duties still kept her in Chaleur and, as Garrison Downs was so far away from the principality, it was impossible for her to have made a quick trip to visit for the weekend as Ana and Connor had done. 'But I'm there in spirit,' she said.

'The Outback princesses of Garrison Downs in their full splendour,' said Connor.

'Without a doubt, the most beautiful sisters in Australia,' said Nate.

'My sisters, the sisters I always dreamed of being with,' said Ana, her voice choked with emotion.

Connor pulled her tight against his chest and dropped a kiss on her mouth.

What had her mother said, back in the dire days of the husband hunt? *Love comes to you when you don't expect it. You have to be open to love for it to find you.*

Love had found her, big-time. Not just the love of Connor, her once-in-a-lifetime love, her husband, the man she adored, her best friend. But also the different kind of love she had found with her sisters.

And she couldn't be happier.

* * * * *

*Look out for the next story in
the One Year to Wed quartet*

Claiming His Billion-Dollar Bride
by Michelle Douglas

And, if you enjoyed this story, check out these other great reads from Kandy Shepherd:

Mistletoe Magic in Tahiti
Pregnancy Shock for the Greek Billionaire
Second Chance with His Cinderella

All available now!